CW00546544

Astral Season, Beastly Season

TAHI SAIHATE

Translated by Kalau Almony

Honford
Star

This translation first published by Honford Star 2020
honfordstar.com
Translation copyright © Kalau Almony 2020
All rights reserved
The moral right of the translator and editors has been asserted.

HOSHI KA KEMONO NI NARU KISETSU
Copyright © Tahi Saihate 2018
English translation rights arranged with CHIKUMASHOBO LTD
through Japan UNI Agency, Inc., Tokyo

ISBN (paperback): 978-1-9162771-0-6
ISBN (ebook): 978-1-9162771-1-3
A catalogue record for this book is available from the British Library.

Printed and bound in Paju, South Korea
Cover design by wangzhihong.com
Typeset by Honford Star
Cover paper: 250 gsm Vent Nouveau by TAKEO
Endleaves: 116 gsm NT Rasha by TAKEO

This book is published with the support of the Japan Foundation.

Contents

Astral Season,
Beastly Season

Dear Mami Aino,

You're cute—that's all you are. You're plain and weak-willed—your friends are the only people in the world to you, and the rest of us are just some shining mass. That's why I could resent you. When you were far away, when you were dancing, I thought I loved you. Why? Why did you kill someone?

It was in my total box of a classroom that suddenly I noticed your name appearing over and over in the glow of my smartphone. On Twitter, on news sites. They said you'd been arrested, which was true.

I looked up when I heard someone ask, "Where's Morishita?" My teacher was looking for my classmate. Class had already started, but he wasn't in the room. He and I had never talked, and I didn't think we'd ever have a conversation or anything, but he was usually there when I went to your shows, and twice we'd made eye contact. Neither of us tried to talk to the other.

Another classmate looked in Morishita's desk and even

raised her hand just to report to our teacher, "His bag isn't here!"

I already knew—he was at the house. I stood up and darted out of class like I was his friend, his good friend.

I went to the bike rack and pulled out my bike.

"Hey, Yamashiro!" My teacher had just managed to catch up. I didn't respond. "Are you feeling sick? What happened to you all of a sudden?"

It was a good thing I'd attended class diligently up till now. My teacher's voice was gentle, and I could even sense a hint of fear. He was probably thinking, *It's such a pain when this kind of student snaps*, or something.

Excuse me. That's all I said.

I got on my bike and my teacher said, "Hey," again, somewhat more forcefully, but I knew he was being a lot softer on me than he'd have been with a delinquent. So I told him about you. That you're cute.

Aino-san is a cute idol. She's the leader of Love You Mixer. She's my age, a junior in high school. Her skin is pale, her hair is dark, and even without special contacts she has two big, round eyes there below her eyebrows. You don't know how many times I've gone to Akihabara for her, to those smoky concert halls. She's cute, but besides the way she looks, there's really nothing special about her. She can only dance and sing because she works hard. It's all just effort. She's an ordinary person who gets by on just effort, and that's why she's so cute, and there's no way that kind of cute person could commit a crime. There's no way she could kill someone, but the news sites and Twitter are filled with messages like, "Underground idol Mami Aino, arrested for suspected murder!" She must be innocent. There's no way she could do something like that. I have to make sure. Are you telling me to die? Are you saying to believe she did it?

I stepped on my bike pedals and sped off.

My teacher was surprised at what I said, and it was easy for me to brush off his hand. I exited the school's front gate and rode down the hill. I tried to brake as little as possible. At some point, the teacher behind me vanished and class resumed. There was no one around the school. I left just like that. It wasn't even afternoon yet, still morning.

I didn't go home. I went straight to your house.

Your house is actually in my neighborhood. Well, you may have been living alone in the city, but I knew you came home once a week. You weren't that busy, and for some reason your family supported you. Maybe they're stupid. You were really cute, but you didn't have much talent, so you had no future in the industry. Your family supported you anyway. There's something cute about that stupidity. It reminds me of you. I acted like I was heading to the park in front of your house and parked my bike. I walked through the forest-like entrance, thick with trees, and sat down on a bench as if I were a salaryman who'd lost his job. I took out my home-made headphone receiver and pulled the antennae up into horns.

"Please, calm down."

"But my daughter couldn't do something like that!"

I could hear the voices through a hidden microphone that seemed to have been placed somewhere in your living room.

"Your daughter's handkerchief was found at the scene of the crime."

"That's impossible!"

"Mom!"

I knew that voice. It was you.

"Did you kill Yu-chan? Tell me the truth."

"That is the truth…"

Of course you'd say something ordinary. You sing songs with such ordinary lyrics, say such normal thank yous when you take pictures with fans after concerts—of course you'd say something ordinary today, too. I held my breath and waited, wondering if I'd be able to hear you breathing. But no matter how hard I strained my ears, all I could hear was cloth rubbing against cloth and footsteps. It would have been nice if whoever hid that microphone put it in a different spot.

Was this "Yu-chan" the little girl who went missing the other day and was then reported murdered? I hadn't seen the news, and I didn't know her name or what she looked like. But recently my mom was going on about something like that. "What's happened to this neighborhood?" she said.

If only Yu-chan got killed by some weirdo. An old man or woman. If only she'd been killed by some freak who just did it for sex or for money. If it was this sort of cliché story, the adults and kids who are into that sort of thing and the internet news updates would vanish so fast they wouldn't even have time to fade away. A new pervert would appear, a new killer would emerge. That would happen over and over, and eventually everyone would just accept it. And then you wouldn't have killed anyone. There'd be no such thing as the killer idol.

Astral Season, Beastly Season

"I killed Yu-chan."

But you said it. I could feel the blood in my veins cloud with bubbles. You were lying. I got this feeling that I had to kill you, strangle you. I had to enact violence on you for lying or else I'd die. I wouldn't be able to keep on living. I'd burst. The bones in my ears were rattling, and my whole body began to resonate along with them. Waveforms crashing and spiking. I had to kill you before I died. And I had to ask you with murderous kindness, murderous righteousness, not to lie. The person who was killed, the body, the corpse, her dreams and hopes and future and passion, all life, I would stomp on it all, crush it, and kill you. Don't lie. I would scream. I needed to let you know. Your color is pink. Pink made from people's bodies ground to dust. It's this texture like my palms, my insides, all my pink parts, spit out. I know. I get it. You're just normal. It's a lie. I know. My opera glasses. I turned to look at you. Into your ears. At your brain. Your thoughts. The pink puddle of your mind. I turned to look into your real eyes.

And then I saw a boy standing pressed up next to your house's fence. Morishita.

Your curtains were closed, so I couldn't see into the house. But Morishita was standing there next to your fence. Morishita who went to your concerts as often as I did.

No one in our class knew Morishita liked idols. No one knew that I liked you specifically, but still the girls would say things like, "I bet you're into idols." I wanted so badly to tell them, *And, what?* but they weren't looking for an answer from me, so I never actually knew what to do. But Morishita was popular, and I'd even seen someone tell him that he looked like some male idol. But he just said, "Who's that?" and the girls laughed at his reply. They laughed. They laughed, and I couldn't hate him either. If he were just moderately condescending to me, if he treated me differently from everyone else, or even if he just acted like he couldn't see me, then it would be easy to hate him. Then I would have justification to hate him, but Morishita always greeted me like he did everyone else, and he didn't date any of the girls in our class, and he even came to your concerts.

The first time I saw him at a show was the first time I went to that concert hall in Shimokitazawa. The other performers weren't idols or anything. I was agonizing over how to even breathe in the middle of all the racket while I waited for your band, Love You Mixer, which was coming on third. Morishita walked up to the bar like it was the natural thing to do, talked a little with the woman working the counter, and got an orange juice. I wondered why he wasn't drinking alcohol, but actually it's because he wasn't drinking alcohol that I realized right away, *Oh, that's Morishita*. At first, I figured he came to see a different band. But he didn't even glance at the second band that was on stage at the time, went straight outside, and came back right before Love You Mixer came on.

You probably don't know, but from the crowd, the stage is brighter than you'd imagine, and the audience's seats are super dark. But because of that, it's also easier to spy on the crowd than you'd expect. I watched Morishita approach the stage slowly, gradually. I never interacted with other fans. I always just watched your shows from the back. But Morishita approached you like it was the natural thing to do. Hold-

ing a pink glowstick. Your color. But your Love You Mixer
fans, even they have a pecking order. That group up front that
cheers for you and has their own strange choreography, they
thought Morishita had to be stopped for ignoring the rules
and trying to get up close. He was actually chased away. He
was shoved by a fat man and got carried all the way to the
edge of the crowd. He seemed shook-up, but he didn't look
even a little angry or irritated. Maybe he's easily intimidated.

He had probably never been to a place like that before.
When the show was over, he left without waiting for any of
the other performers. I thought about telling him that after
the show he could meet you and take pictures, but I wasn't
sure if he had noticed me. It would have been a bother to go
out of the way just to tell him I was there, so I let him leave.

After that, he was always at the shows I went to. He gradually began to understand the rules and would stand behind
the people dancing, where he could see best. I stood behind
him so I could stare at you without him noticing.

Morishita was up against your fence, probably eavesdropping like me. Or maybe from that close he could hear actual
screaming and shouting. I didn't have the courage to go and
try to listen. Morishita looked strange, standing completely
still with his body pressed to the fence like a lizard. I was right,
though. When I heard he wasn't in class, I knew he'd be here.

There were three cars in front of the house, probably all
police cars. The incident happened nearby, so I knew where
they'd take you. Morishita probably knew, too.

"How could you do that?"

"I killed Yu-chan, cut him up, and laid out the pieces like

a star. I did it under the tree at the power spot at the Azaya-ma Shrine. The one that TV crew visited the other day. He looked cute, I thought."

"If that's the case, we'll be taking your daughter to the station."

I could hear it all in my headphones. Your words were calm but so cheap, they had to have been lies.

Do you understand? Do you really get it? Yu-chan was killed, cut up, and left under a tree at some "power spot," some place the media claimed to have special spiritual energy to draw idiot tourists. If you say you did it, I won't be able to look down on you for being plain. Don't you see? You can't be so evil. You should just keep on learning your stupid songs and dances through sheer effort. Isn't that the kind of person you are?

Before you were taken from your home, I got on my bike and sped out of there. Morishita was already gone. He may have been hiding somewhere. But he knew I liked you, and I didn't mind being seen by him. My bike went faster, faster, faster. I would speed down the hill, and then when I got to the bottom, I wouldn't be able to make the turn and I'd crash and die. It seemed like my heart would burst if I didn't imagine that for the full minute I was descending. There's no way someone like you could be a murderer. There's no way.

Blood. I've never seen blood. Well, I've seen the dribbles of blood that flows out of small wounds, but that's it. I've never had an operation. If possible, I'd like to never have to see someone die. When cute girls wear makeup that doesn't suit

Astral Season, Beastly Season

them just because some model promotes it, and that makeup actually makes them ugly, I want to tell them that they're ugly. And if those girls get embarrassed, I think that'd be great. I want to walk down Takeshita Street in Harajuku looking down on everyone. I'll wear secret platform shoes.

I made the turn and arrived home without crashing. I thought about it and realized it'd be bad if my parents found out I left school early, so I grabbed my dog, Hana, and went for a walk.

You probably don't know where my house is, but it takes about five minutes to get there from your place by bike. It's on the exact opposite side of the park. And from there, if you go straight north, there's a small river. On days there isn't much water, wild boars walk around there. Hana started barking at one.

"Hey, Yamashiro!"

It wasn't a boar that responded to Hana's barking, but someone walking by. Morishita. He was standing there looking like he just ditched school and went to an arcade.

Morishita asked me, "Why aren't you in school?" He didn't mention that he was skipping too. I told him quietly that I had an emergency.

"Me too," he said. I noticed then that there was a little girl standing next to him. When I asked, Who's she? he said, "My little sister. She's cute, isn't she?"

I didn't feel like responding. Just her bangs were tied up with a rubber band with a bear on it. She kind of looked a bit like you, but I'm not sure she was cute. Maybe I'll send you a picture later. He didn't try to talk to me about you at all. Even though I'm pretty sure he noticed me at your concerts. Then he said, "Let's both do our best," smiling.

That night that girl's face kept showing up on the news. She was missing. There was no ransom request or any contact. They said she was last seen wearing a rubber band with a bear on it. That this case resembled the previous one. That a suspect, Girl A, was already in police custody. I was eating chocolate. It was a bit early for it, but the heated *kotatsu* table was already out in the living room. I asked my mom for a café au lait, and she brought me one. While I drank it, I heard her say, "How disgusting."

Maybe it's because murdered girls genuinely look beautiful, or maybe it's just because I'm a boy, but I think there must be something enjoyable about having all these delusions about the opposite sex and living to force a sort of bodily aesthetics one could never pull off themselves onto others. Apparently, the police claimed there were similarities to the previous case that had not yet been made public, so they were advancing their investigation carefully.

You still hadn't been released. You confessed like an idiot. The search of your house must have ended fruitlessly. But there was never any follow-up report. What happened after that? I keep seeing that question on Twitter. There are strange rumors about you and comments from girls claiming to be your classmates, but it's all lies. I've looked into it, so I know, but those kinds of sites are filled with more lies than you can even imagine. Still, there are people who can just believe that stuff.

Astral Season, Beastly Season

The next day when I went to school, my homeroom teacher put his hands on his hips and called me over. Just before I asked what was wrong, I remembered that I ran off unexcused yesterday.

"I contacted your parents."

But my mom didn't say anything. I wonder why. My mom hasn't said anything to me for a long time. Not that it really matters.

I'm sorry. That's all I said.

"Next time this happens, you're going to the principal's office." Why did he pick such an ineffective line?

What about Morishita?

"He'll be going to the principal's next time, too."

Is he here today?

"He pretty much always shows up at the last minute."

He's not staying home today?

"What happened? I haven't heard anything about him missing class."

I wanted to know what kind of face he'd make when he came to school. Do you have any idea how much Morishita put my mind at ease? Maybe you don't realize, but Morishita probably killed that girl. He must have killed Yu-chan, too. I was sure. You were innocent, and your obvious plainness was beginning to expose itself. What peace of mind! When I saw Morishita, I would tell him to let me help, too.

Morishita showed up just before class started and began greeting everyone almost at random. He even made eye contact with me and said, "Good morning," or something. Was he an idiot? One of our classmates was asking if he watched Music Station yesterday, and he did, while I was watching the news about that girl.

"Want to go to that place again after school?" someone asked him. "It's been a while since we've gone." Morishita said he was busy. That's right. I'm going to be busy too. Class started.

Two children had been killed. I figured that meant high schoolers like us wouldn't have to run around worrying about being attacked, but our teacher told us to go home in groups. I ignored him, but my classmates seemed to take the whole thing really seriously. They were all talking about who they'd go home with. I panicked and went up to Morishita. "What?" asked another one of our classmates near him, surprised. But I figured if Morishita and I didn't promise to leave together, it would be difficult for me to help him. I assumed that if I asked him to walk home with me, no one else would.

Umm, will you walk home with me?

Morishita immediately said, "Sure," smiling.

"What? Seriously?" said a girl. But I ignored her. Morishita ignored her, too.

When I headed back to my seat, my leg got caught on someone else's and I almost fell. "Watch out," said the guy who tripped me. He did it on purpose, I thought, but I didn't say anything.

Standing next to Morishita, it was really obvious how tall he was. Next to his slim figure, I felt like a soccer ball. School was over. Morishita wasn't in any clubs or anything either, and he turned down all the invitations from other classmates to hang out. We were heading home, just me and Morishita. I tried to be brave. I tried to be brave, but we left the school gates and headed down the hill. Morishita had both his hands on the back of his head and was looking up at the sky. He didn't look like he was trying to say anything or waiting for me to bring anything up.

Morishita, I said.

"Yeah?"

I didn't think I could say anything else, but Morishita finally looked at me.

Mami's been arrested, I said.

"Yeah," he said, like we had always been your fan friends. He continued. "I hope they let her out soon."

Yeah. I agreed with Morishita. I wanted someone to prove as soon as possible how innocent, how helpless you are. Anyone. The real criminal. Yes, even Morishita.

Can I help you? I asked.

"With what?"

Killing. Come on. You killed that girl yesterday, didn't you? I heard they found her at another power spot.

"Yeah, I did."

I figured, but… That was seriously you?

"I mean, you asked."

Yeah, and…

"Do it."

What?

"Help me." Morishita was smiling. I wonder if his smile looked like there was just a bit of evil mixed up in it because he had a beautiful face. Beautiful people look a bit like demons or monsters. "I figured I should do another one today."

Yeah?

"But before that, I thought I'd stop by the house again." He was talking about your family's house. He had gone yesterday but was going to go again today.

Why? Is something gonna happen today?

"No, I doubt it. Even if something does happen, it'll probably just be an emergency call from the police or something. It's so hard just sitting there waiting for something to happen, so yesterday, I set up a tape recorder."

Oh. To record the broadcast from that weird hidden mic?

"Yeah. You know about that too?"

Let me explain. I didn't hide that microphone and neither did Morishita. Have you ever gotten a present from a fan and taken it home? The mic was probably hidden in there. After checking a bunch of frequencies near your house, I picked that one up. I was able to listen to you just because I got lucky, and I'm sure Morishita did the same.

You started recording it? I asked.

"Yeah," he said. "I'm going to check what's there. There might be some good information." He thought that since another kid was killed in that same way, the police might start to suspect your parents. "I did it just like she said. I chopped her up and laid the pieces out in the shape of a star. It seems like the only people who know about that are the criminal and the police. But Mami said that all right in front of her parents, right? So it wouldn't be strange if the police figure that her parents killed that girl to cover up their daughter's crime."

Astral Season, Beastly Season

That day, I didn't take my bike. I didn't want to get in Morishita's way, so I left it at home. He lived a five-minute walk from school, and I'd never seen him on a bike. We walked together to your house.

It took fifteen minutes. Summer was ending, but walking was way more tiring than biking, and I started to sweat.

Morishita went straight into the park without saying anything. It seems he had hid his recording device in some bushes. He told me, "Keep look out," and went to search for it. He pulled out a small voice recorder and some strange device he'd made from circuits. The setup was in a blue plastic box. He pulled out another voice recorder, switched the two, and returned the box, all very efficiently.

But, I said. But won't the police find that soon?

"Good. I want them to find it."

Why?

"If they find it, that'd mean I committed all the crimes and framed Mami-chan."

But if they just think you're eavesdropping, none of that will mean anything.

"Huh?"

If they find it after you become a possible suspect, that'd be one thing. But if they don't suspect you at all, they'll just think it's a prank or something. Mami-chan is an idol after all.

"You're right... But I still want to know about their investigation."

Don't worry, I said, nodding. Morishita's eyes sparked, and he grabbed my hand. Let's bury it, I said. Then we can record it with a smartphone. That way we can broadcast the recording 24-hours a day.

"But the phone's battery will die."

I'll go to Akihabara and buy an extra battery pack. We'll attach it, then bury that along with a fan so it doesn't overheat. And we should use a metal box instead. We'll need a bigger space.

"What? You'll do all that?"

I nodded again. Morishita shook my hand almost violently, but he seemed happy.

"Thank you!" he said. He must not have been good with electronics. Either way, I would make sure we could properly eavesdrop on your house. I just had to go to Akihabara to get the parts we'd need.

"While you're doing that," Morishita said, "I think I'll kill someone else."

Who? And was that girl yesterday really your sister?

"No, no. That was her friend," he said. "I figured it'd be best to go for people I have connections with so the police can track me down eventually. I knew the first victim, too."

Really?

I hadn't properly researched the first case. After all, I didn't think you'd actually get arrested, and your shows were more important than that murder. I had to remember to stock up on glow sticks.

"But who should I kill? I have an idea. Tonight… Do you know that place, Sato's Sweets?" Morishita asked out of the blue. I shook my head. "One of the girls in our class found this place recently. Their green tea parfaits are really good.

Astral Season, Beastly Season

Ha, you look surprised. I don't like sweets, but Japanese-style ones are all right. Anyway, I'm supposed to meet someone there tonight."

And you're going to kill them?

"Yeah," Morishita answered calmly. I wished he was at least a little excited or hesitant. I didn't want to be there at the actual scene, so I explained how getting everything in Akihabara would be a long errand.

"Don't worry. I'll take care of the killing."

Morishita sounded just like a member of some committee taking on a project. Still, I decided to go along with what he said.

It takes an hour and twenty minutes to get to Akihabara by train, so I really did need Morishita to take care of the killing. I squeezed the hanging strap on the train tight, as if to crush the sweat beading on my hand, and thought to myself that next time I'd do my part and help him kill. I was standing, and across from me there was a girl sitting, staring at me. She was wearing my school's uniform. When I turned my eyes away, she got up and approached me. "Hey, Yamashiro."

I had heard that voice in class this morning. It was the girl who said, "Seriously?" or something. One of Morishita's followers. When I looked her straight in the face close up, I could see that she had thick makeup on around her eyes.

"What, are you going to cram school, too?"

What was her name? Watase or something like that. I shook my head.

"Oh, really?"

Umm, Watase-san?

"Yes?"

Aren't you different in school? I asked. She usually seemed like, like she just wanted everything she didn't care about to die. And like she'd even been granted permission to feel that way.

"Yeah, girls turn really evil when they get together. It must be that. Are you scared of me?"

No, not scared.

When Watase smiled you could see her pointy canines sticking out.

"But we've never talked, right? So don't say such mean things."

Sure.

"So, if you don't have cram school, where are you going?"

I didn't have the courage to say I was going to Akihabara. I just played dumb and said, Umm.

"All right," she said, looking satisfied.

So you go to cram school?

"Yeah."

Lots of our classmates go to cram school, but there's a big one in the shopping area near our school—not that many kids take the train into the city.

"Today I have English class," Watase explained. "The school's famous for their teaching methods."

Famous? Really? So why do you go there?

"My older brother and sister both went there, and they got into the University of Tokyo. I guess it's kind of set up for the University of Tokyo's English exam."

Astral Season, Beastly Season

You want to go to the University of Tokyo? When I asked, I must have made a face like I was making fun of her, or more like I was surprised, like the one I made when Morishita talked about eating green tea parfaits. But Watase just looked straight at me and said, "Yeah. I want to make robots to take care of elderly people. Oh, does that surprise you? You know I do pretty well in school."

Oh, yeah?

"I'm always in the top three in the class for test scores."

I guess I have seen your name a lot. But I always thought it was the boy Watase. Your name's written with the Chinese character for "bright" isn't it? I guess it is a u-unisex name.

"It's a great name, isn't it?" Watase showed her canines again.

I could see the sun setting through the window. It looked like the town was in flames.

"It kind of looks like a fire, doesn't it?" Watase whispered, just as the thought crossed my mind. I couldn't say anything in reply. What would Morishita have said? "They say that at the age of seventeen, you either become a star or a beast. It was in my English reading for today." Watase's profile reflected the fiery light. "It said you stop being human and become either a star or a beast for a while. Adults say really terrible things, don't they?" The sun lit up the mountain and gradually faded pink.

Watase, do you like Morishita? Something drew me into asking that question.

"What? No," she answered instantly. "You know that guy, Aoyama? He's always hanging around Morishita. I like him.

Oh, I should say, I only said that because it's you."

Yikes.

"You don't have anyone to tell that to."

So cold! I didn't respond, and Watase's expression gradually returned to the bored look she always had in class. At the next stop, she rushed off the train.

I spent the next forty minutes transferring from rattling train to rattling train. I arrived at Akihabara, and then went home. I buried my setup in the park. I should have gotten Morishita's number. I couldn't tell if anything happened or not. There was nothing on the news. The Japanese sweets place must have closed by now.

As soon as I got to class the next morning, I needed to see this Aoyama, so I looked at the seating chart. He sat behind Morishita. Morishita wasn't there yet of course. More importantly, it seemed like nothing had happened last night, but was that really the case? After a while, Aoyama showed up. As soon as he entered the classroom, he started talking to a classmate and laughing like an idiot. He didn't take his seat, but the people around him were calling him Aoyama, so it must have been him. He was definitely one of the people surrounding Morishita yesterday. He was the one who tripped me.

He said, "Good morning" to no one in particular, sat down, and let out a massive yawn. Right then, Morishita showed up, earlier than usual.

"Hey, Aoyama." Morishita didn't say good morning to everyone like he always did. He went straight to Aoyama and grabbed him by the collar.

Astral Season, Beastly Season

"What's wrong, Mori?"

"Why didn't you come yesterday?"

"What? You're mad about that? Sorry."

"You just cancel at the last minute, and that's all you have to say?"

Morishita punched Aoyama in the face. Aoyama landed on his butt. Girls yelled. The classroom grew loud.

"What? This is seriously weird. You not feeling well, Mori?" Still Aoyama didn't seem mad, more like shocked. Maybe it was Aoyama who Morishita had agreed to get green tea parfaits with. If that were the case, then to Aoyama, Morishita looked like he was flying into a rage over a broken promise to get a snack. That *would* be shocking.

"That hurt, you know."

"Shut up!"

Morishita threw himself into his seat without so much as helping Aoyama up. Even the girls who always flocked to Morishita just watched him from a distance today. Watase ran to Aoyama. I stopped watching after that.

Our teacher showed up soon after and called Morishita and Aoyama up to the front. Watase told him she wanted to take Aoyama to the nurse's first, so only Morishita got sent to the principal's. Still after that the girls started saying things like, "I wonder if Morishita will be all right?" They're so oblivious.

Morishita came back right away. First period began. Aoyama hadn't returned. It was a good excuse, so he probably figured he could use it to skip. After first period ended, Watase showed up by herself looking worried. She walked over to Morishita and said, "Hey."

"What?"

"You should apologize to Aoyama."

"This has nothing to do with you."

"I don't know what happened with you two, but you can't just hit people."

It was break time, but while Morishita and Watase were at it, the classroom was silent. They were not their usual selves. I saw Morishita giving this awful grin. It was different from his regular smile. He looked like he was laughing at someone.

"Watase, you like Aoyama…"

Morishita! I yelled. I grabbed his arm. In that moment all the eyes in the class fell on me. Watase looked at me, surprised, but it didn't matter. I didn't care what she thought of me.

"I'm sorry," said Morishita.

All I wanted was to stop Morishita. I don't know if that got across to him, but the second he looked at my face, he apologized. His voice was quiet, and Watase didn't respond. I wished class would start already.

During our next break and during lunch, no one talked to Morishita. It was easy to walk home together today, too. After school we climbed down the hill in silence.

"I'm sorry. I shouldn't have dragged you into that."

It's fine, I said, shaking my head. I didn't have the courage to ask about the details.

"Yesterday, I thought I'd go to that café with Aoyama, but he didn't come so I couldn't kill him."

So you were planning to? To kill Aoyama?

"You know, we're close and everything. I just made that

scene in class now, too. So I figure if Aoyama dies or something, they'll probably suspect me."

Was that seriously his goal? To make himself the suspect when Aoyama died? Even though it would upset Watase so much?

Morishita nodded like he understood what I was thinking. "It would be awful for Watase."

It wouldn't be so bad, would it?

"You know she likes Aoyama, right?"

Yeah.

"If you don't want me to kill Aoyama for Watase's sake, I'll think about it."

But I didn't say anything. After all, whoever dies, whoever's sad about those deaths, that will never compare to the wounds you caused me. I have to prove to the world that you truly are normal.

"Oh, also, about the recording," Morishita whispered like he suddenly remembered. He took home the voice recorder after we collected it yesterday. "It seems the police are still considering the second killing a copycat crime. Mami's mother talked with them on the phone a few times, but it sounds like she's not getting released anytime soon."

Even though she's innocent, I said, kicking the sand at my feet.

"Really? Is she?" Morishita's voice suddenly went high. "She's innocent? Seriously?"

She must be! That kind of person couldn't have killed anyone!

"Do you have proof? Do you?"

Seeing how excited he was, I realized that it wasn't Morishita who committed the first murder. My hope that the true criminal was Morishita began to vanish. And I learned that, until this moment, he believed you really killed someone, and still he went so far as to kill that little girl to try and make you look innocent.

"I see," Morishita said in response to my silence.

It's all because you acted like you were someone different. Because you acted like a weirdo to get people's attention. But Morishita still sounded relieved when he whispered, "That's great." He went on. "If Mami-chan's really innocent, then they'll definitely let her go if we just keep trying. It's so sad that she's locked up. But you said there's no evidence?"

Yeah...

"Well, we just have to keep going with the copycat killings."

What Morishita meant was there seemed to be a theory circulating among the police that because the information that the body in the first crime was cut up and arranged in a star pattern still hadn't been released to the public, no copycat killer would know that. Therefore only the real criminal would dismember their victim that way. But if the real criminal was on the loose, that still left the question, *How did you know about the body of the first victim?* We needed something definitive to prove someone else committed the first crime. I told Morishita about the police mentioning your handkerchief. Apparently, he heard, too. That was their material evidence.

"That's all? If we stole a few things and left them at the crime scenes, we could fake as many crimes as we wanted.

Astral Season, Beastly Season

Why did Mami-chan get arrested for something so trivial?"

I was silent.

"That's it, Yamashiro!" Morishita called my name in his usual cheerful voice. When I looked him in the eyes he smiled faintly. "Let's steal something! Some of her things. And then we'll leave them at the murder scenes."

What? I asked, but it seemed like Morishita had already made up his mind. His steps suddenly became lighter, and then he turned the corner onto the big road to head to your house.

"If they knew it was Mami-chan's handkerchief, she must have gotten her name embroidered on it somewhere. How cute. Yamashiro, how are your PE grades?"

I shook my head. I was depressingly unathletic.

"I see. I'm not sure I can pull off a burglary either."

Besides, there are probably cops watching Mami's house. She is a murder suspect. We shouldn't do anything stupid.

"But it'd be fine if they catch me, right?"

Not yet. If they find out you were trying to plant evidence to show that Mami-chan's innocent, they'll just suspect her even more.

"I guess you're right."

Morishita stopped walking. He looked like he was thinking. Sneaking into your house would probably be straightforward. Someone got that hidden microphone in there so easily—you must not have been very attentive to security. But it's not like we were professional thieves.

"I got it! Yamashiro, do you know that Okayama guy? The old dude who's always dancing in the front row at Mami-chan's concerts?" He's a bald, skinny old man. Even you probably know who he is. He was always at your concerts.

"I'm not sure, but he's probably the one who snuck the microphone into her house. I've seen him there a bunch when I went nearby to listen. I'm sure he lives in the city, so he's going out of his way to come here."

So what?

"I wouldn't put it past him to have stolen some of her things. I've contacted him a couple of times for tickets, and I've got his phone number."

You know him?

"Yeah. But even just buying a ticket off him, he made a big deal of it and made me show him my school ID. But because of that, I'm sure he's got a record of me."

I didn't realize then why Morishita was saying that.

Morishita began walking to the station without saying anything to me. I knew it was to rob Okayama's house, but did Morishita know where he lived? When I asked he said, "I don't, but he's following this other idol group, so if we stake out their show tonight we'll probably find him."

You want to tail him? Morishita nodded, smiling. And with just that, I was relieved. We'd be going all the way to Akihabara, so that meant Morishita wouldn't try to kill Aoyama today. I didn't care if he killed him eventually, but I guess I wasn't ready for that yet.

I looked around the train car, but Watase wasn't there. She must not have been going to her English cram school today. I decided to ask Morishita if he was going to go to college, and

Astral Season, Beastly Season

if he was going to cram school. I really just meant it as small talk.

"I'm not going. I quit all that. There was no point."

I'm pretty sure Morishita had good grades. Decently good ones. I had decently bad ones, and I used to think that was the difference between competent and incompetent people.

"What about you?"

When I said I don't go to cram school, Morishita replied, "Yeah, we're busy supporting Mami-chan." His response came so easily.

You quit cram school for Mami-chan?

"Yeah. I had originally been going to Akihabara for cram school, so I do owe discovering her to them. But I never really saw the point in going, so it's good I found something else to focus on."

Morishita, aren't you worried about the future?

"Why would I be? I'm just going to jail anyway."

I stopped myself as I was about to say, *But…*

I wasn't really studying. I just liked you. I couldn't do anything. My shapeless spirit flittered inside me, and my skin began to heat up from the inside out.

"It doesn't matter what happens. I don't care if I die, if I'm killed, if I get caught. As long as I can save Mami-chan, it doesn't matter what happens. That's why I'm alive. It doesn't matter if I have a future, if I have a life beyond that. I don't care about any of that."

Sitting next to him, I felt my shoulders stiffen just slightly. I wanted to ask, *Wasn't it meaningless to live a life like that? Supported by only Mami-chan?* But for some reason I thought it would feel bad to hurt his feelings. You're the one who gave him all those half-assed dreams. I had to show him that you were just an ordinary person, the kind you could find anywhere.

Morishita, what do you like about Mami-chan?

"I like that she's cute and a good dancer."

But she's just practicing as hard as she can. She doesn't have any talent.

"That's what's best about her."

I get that. That's why you're great. Because you have absolutely no talent, no sense, and yet you work so hard to act like you do despite your inferiority complex. Your favorite food, your favorite music, it's all so normal, so you're proud of anything that's slightly different about yourself. It's that attitude, that pathetic attempt to be even just a little bit better than others that I love. What I mean is, you're sad and pathetic, so I can look down on you however much I want.

"Being hardworking is a kind of talent, too," Morishita mumbled. Suddenly Watase's face appeared in my mind. "I liked watching her work hard. Dancing, singing on stage like she's having fun. I was trying hard, too. I thought I was trying hard. But then there was someone else trying harder than me, and still, she was having fun. When I realized that, I had no choice but to like her. I wanted to do my best, my absolute best, to cheer her on. She's special."

I couldn't tell him, *That's wrong.* I stared from the train window at the ads on the buildings we passed. Did you dream of being up there, right in the center? Did you want to make millions? Make cell phone ring tones?

Astral Season, Beastly Season

The pupils of Morishita's eyes were like a pair of deep holes. When I saw him with that little girl he was going to kill, I hadn't yet noticed either his willingness to kill or his dedication.

"We're here."

Morishita stood up, and I rushed after him. Akihabara station was the same as always.

Are you friends with a lot of other fans? I asked as we walked through the bustle of Akihabara. It was already early evening. It was also a weekday, so even just a little off the main road the number of people dropped drastically.

"I am. We even hang out after concerts and stuff. But Okayama never came. He liked being alone. You too, right?" I didn't even know they had those kinds of fan meetups. I had never talked to other fans. I got all my information on the internet.

But you still managed to get in contact with the lone wolf Okayama?

"It wasn't such a big deal. I just got him to scalp me tickets."

We arrived at a small concert hall underneath a maid café. The names of idol groups were listed up on a chalkboard in front. I had seen all those names before, but none of them were particularly popular groups.

"Let's just wait outside. I'm pretty sure Okayama follows this group, Barely Ribbon. If this is the lineup, he should come out within an hour."

But would he really be going to a show now? An idol he likes from a different group just killed someone.

"I don't know, but Okayama's that kind of guy. It's a little strange, but he's got a lot of favorites."

Morishita relayed that information calmly and headed to a convenience store. I guess he planned on pretending to browse magazines while we watched for Okayama. After about an hour, Okayama did leave that concert hall. And he was alone.

"He moves alone like that 'cause it's easier to steal their things that way," Morishita said as he returned a magazine about TV shows to the rack. He patted me on the shoulder and dashed out of the store. I hurried after him. Okayama seemed to be heading back to Akihabara station. It was already dark. He walked along the mostly-deserted roads without paying any mind to his surroundings. All I could do was follow along silently as Morishita tailed Okayama. I could see nothing besides Morishita's back. I couldn't even see Okayama.

The two of them were fast walkers. My heartbeat sounded like footsteps. I was out of breath, and the thumping reverberated in my eardrums. Keep up, keep up. I wasn't even sure what I was doing anymore. Even though the two people in front of me were walking with such conviction. My legs stopped moving. Morishita's figure receded. I wondered if he'd even notice if I just went home right now. For you, Morishita would steal, he would kill. I wanted to show that you didn't kill anyone, too. But I couldn't be like Morishita. I was tired. My body hurt. I was sleepy. I didn't want to walk anymore. I didn't care about any crime.

"Yamashiro!" Someone was pulling on my arm. When I looked up, Morishita was right in front of me. "Are you all right?"

Astral Season, Beastly Season

Oh, I'm sorry… I…

"It's okay. I saw which platform Okayama went to. The train's coming in four minutes. Let's hurry."

I realized there was a train station right in front of me. Jack o' lanterns were lined up in front of a cake shop. It was fall. I saw that it was already fall, and also that Morishita probably hadn't even noticed that. I wondered if something would go wrong and he'd die. He would probably be okay with that. But I wasn't ready to accept it.

"Let's go, Yamashiro."

I nodded and headed to the platform with Morishita.

Okayama was wearing a thin coat and had his hands in his pockets the whole time. His coat was wrinkled and splotchy, like it was still wet in spots from not getting dried out properly. Morishita and I pretended to be high school kids from the country visiting Akihabara.

"That maid café was great, wasn't it?"

Totally.

"Let's go again next time."

It felt strange to talk with Morishita like we were friends. Do Aoyama and Watase ever get this calm feeling? There was something really comforting about that, about being friends with someone that no one makes fun of, who everyone likes. I didn't want to become that kind of person though. When Morishita smiles, his brow wrinkles just a bit, like something tickles. He really looks like a kid. Seeing that, I knew he had probably never worried at all about laughing, being surprised, raising his voice. But I didn't want to be like him. I didn't want to know what kind of loneliness and hate he actually felt. I wanted to become like his stupid friends, the ones who truly believe that he's really just a good guy.

The train arrived. We made sure Okayama got on, and then we boarded from the next door over. He was moving his hands around in his pockets. Morishita told me under his breath, "He probably stole something again." He was far away and likely couldn't hear us. This whole time I had really wanted to ask why Morishita decided on Okayama as his next target.

"I've seen him do it a bunch. He stole a mechanical pencil from her bag. Another time I saw him take a straw and a tissue she used to wipe her mouth and put them in plastic bags."

How did you see that? You'd have to get backstage.

"Well…" Morishita looked embarrassed. "I don't want to admit it, but actually, a few times, I put on a staff pass and snuck into the back."

When they were performing with boy bands?

"What? How did you know?"

With his looks, Morishita definitely could've snuck in.

"I thought about stealing, too," he whispered. "I'd be happy with some trash. I'd be happy with anything. I wanted to make whatever it was into a kind of good luck charm. But Okayama just looked so pathetic doing that, so I stopped myself. I'm pretty sure Mami-chan even noticed. But she just kept smiling and shaking hands with fans. She's so nice."

She's just oblivious, I wanted to say. But I wasn't sure why I wanted to say that.

The train arrived at Osaki station. Okayama shoved people

out of the way as he got off. We rushed off the train as well.

I heard Morishita say, "Mami-chan lives around this station."

I didn't know this is where you lived. Only Okayama and Morishita knew that. I think they probably did something shady to find that out. Did you think no one knew about you? As soon as we left the station, we crossed a river. Fallen leaves were probably drifting along there, but it was already dark out, and I couldn't even make out the river's surface. Just one spot shined sharply with the breaking of little waves. Something must have been floating there. I hoped it was something natural. Morishita kept a bit of distance from Okayama so he wouldn't be noticed. We crossed the river then followed it along, then we came to a park, and after cutting through the park, we arrived at a nice apartment building. I was told by Morishita that you lived there. Right across the street there's another, rundown apartment building, right? The one where the first-floor corner apartment always has dirty towels out drying over the brick wall? Apparently, that's where Okayama lived. Maybe he's even snuck into your room before.

After watching to see which room Okayama went into, Morishita asked, "Yamashiro, what are you going to do?" He didn't turn to look at me.

What?

"Are you gonna go home? I'm gonna wait for Okayama to go back out."

W-wait. It's already late.

"Okayama doesn't look particularly healthy, and he didn't

buy anything to eat after the concert. I don't think his day's over yet. When we talked before, he only replied late at night."

But...

"It seems more likely things'll work out if I wait for him, so I'm not going anywhere. Maybe you should go home. You haven't told your parents where you are, have you?"

Yeah, I said. But I didn't have the courage to just leave.

Morishita, I'll wait for the last train.

"Really?"

There are still almost three hours. I patted Morishita on the shoulder. If we just stand here, someone will report us to the police.

"That's fine. Oh, but, that's right. If we're found out now, we won't be able to save Mami-chan."

Yeah... Morishita, do you have a smart phone?

I took his phone and stuck mine into one of the gaps in the brick wall across the street from Okayama's building. I adjusted the camera so we could see the door to Okayama's apartment and changed the settings on Morishita's phone.

"What are you doing?"

We're going to use my phone as a surveillance camera. We can use this to watch what happens from a store close by. That way we don't have to stay here.

"Is that okay? Are you just going to leave your phone there like that?"

It's fine, I said. The truth is, since you'd been arrested, I hadn't had anything to look up on my phone.

We watched several people come and go from the apartment building, but Okayama didn't make any moves. Morishita and I were sharing French fries at a fast food restaurant. He stared at the screen of his phone.

"If he doesn't leave today, what should we do? Should we just break in?"

Why?

"We've got to hurry. If we don't, Mami-chan will get sent to prison."

I guess you were still in the holding cell at the local police bureau. Morishita said they'd take you to a real prison soon.

"Ah!" Morishita shouted at the screen. When I looked, I saw a shadowy figure leaving from the door Okayama had gone in to. It was too dark to really make out who it was, but it had to be Okayama. Before I could move, Morishita stood up and rushed out of the restaurant.

As soon as we arrived in front of Okayama's apartment, Morishita handed me plastic bags and rubber bands. He told me to wrap my hands and feet. "I'm going in through the window. You come in after I open the front door." I looked, and the window on the side of Okayama's apartment was open. If Morishita climbed over the brick wall, he could get in.

But doesn't that mean Okayama's coming right back?

"He probably doesn't bother locking up because he doesn't have anything valuable."

Morishita ignored my concern and climbed right over the wall. I had no choice but to hurry to the door.

The door opened right away. At Morishita's signal, I entered the room. There was a completely unused kitchen right in front of me, and beyond that, a small tatami room. It stank of mold. Okayama's clothes were piled up on top of bags of trash, and I could barely see the floor. Morishita quickly pointed beneath the bed and took out a small box. On the box, "Okayama Mami" was written in ballpoint pen. I guess you two were married in his head. Morishita opened that box, and in contrast with the room, inside were plastic bags arranged frighteningly neatly. On the corner of each was a date, and they were organized chronologically. Tissues, straws, a spoon. There was a handkerchief, some stationary, a hair clip. Even one of the wrist bands that, for a time, all the members of Love You Mixer used to wear.

Maybe to tell yours apart from the others', your name was written on there, too.

"Let's go with this," Morishita said, taking the wrist band. Then, silently, he also pulled out two plastic bags with tissues inside.

I wanted to ask if he really needed those, but I had no idea where all this murder would end.

Morishita and I returned the box and prepared to go. And then we heard a phone ring. It was coming from under the duvet on the bed. The display said SHOP. Maybe it was Okayama's work place or something? Without any hesitation, Morishita picked up the smart phone. The second the ringing ended, he tried to unlock the phone. He input your birthday as the password and the phone unlocked.

"Look at that."

Morishita showed me a picture. It was of you standing on stage. The picture was taken from a pretty low angle, and we could see the pannier under your skirt.

Astral Season, Beastly Season

"I guess he was into taking pervy pictures."

We looked through the photos on his phone, and it was nothing but a bunch of pictures like that of a lot of different girls. When I turned away, Morishita whispered, "He's gross." But then, I heard him say, "What's this?"

"Yamashiro, isn't this Mami-chan's handwriting?" He showed me pictures of pages from some sort of notebook. The handwriting certainly looked like yours. Each entry was dated, so it must have been a journal. Morishita took a picture of each page with his own phone camera.

Morishita, we should go.

He ignored me. But Okayama would be back soon.

In the end, it turned out I was worrying about the wrong thing. Right after he finished taking photos, we heard the gurgling of the toilet flush. And then, from behind us, came the cheerful voice of a girl. "Are you my brother's friends?" The moment I heard that voice, Morishita stood up and pushed the girl down. I turned and all I could see was the girl's legs and Morishita on top of her. White socks that came up to her knees. She must have been young.

Morishita, what are you doing? Stop!

Could he not hear me? He was totally still. I couldn't hear the girl. In that moment I didn't even imagine that girl was being strangled.

Maybe I screamed. Maybe that's the one thing I didn't do. Next thing I do know, I had run from that room. I had climbed down the stairs and run all the way to the nearby park. I thought Morishita might follow me, but he didn't try to contact me. I was scared. I was scared, so I went and got my phone, and headed straight to the station. I didn't want to see Morishita. And he didn't try to call me or anything either. The town was so quiet. No one left your apartment building. Not even a single person in Okayama's apartment building came out of their room. No one noticed the unusual goings on. Light drifted down the river like *somen* noodles. That was the only thing that looked the same as before. My heart had probably climbed up to the back of my eyes. They stung to the rhythm of my heartbeat.

I jumped onto a train. I watched Osaki pass by. There was a dead body there—Morishita was there. What did he do? What will he do? Morishita might even cut up that body. Will the cops find it tomorrow? Is Morishita angry?

All we were trying to do is prove that you couldn't have killed anyone. We just wanted to prove that you were normal. Morishita had already killed two people. I ran away when I saw it happening. Did I not actually realize what was happening? Didn't I realize the moment Morishita shoved that girl over, that she was going to die? What should I do? Should I have stopped Morishita? If I had, that girl would have figured out that we were thieves. Could I let that happen? If I had, it could have come to light that we were trying to fake your innocence. I couldn't let that happen. I had to let that girl die for you.

I got off the train at the station Watase got off at the day before. She probably wouldn't be going to cram school there today, I thought. There were other subjects she had to study besides English. I sat completely still on a platform bench and thought about her. I didn't have a photo of her, and I barely remembered her face. How would she feel if Morishita killed Aoyama? Would she hate me a little if I was involved? For some reason, that thought had this heart-crushing weight to it. I didn't want Watase to ignore me. When I think about it now, I was happy she had talked to me. Bite down. Watase will definitely forget about that soon. The day before was the only time we'd ever talked. I'd be happy if she remembered me even vaguely in ten years—that would be enough for me. She'll probably forget. Well then, I should make her hate me then. But I couldn't bring myself to think that. I'm so pathetic that I couldn't make myself feel that if she was going to forget me anyway, she might as well hate me. I'm worthless to my very soul.

The last train was announced and slid up in front of me. I worried whether Morishita was already on it, but of course he wasn't. There were several missed calls from my parents, but instead of returning them I just sent a text. A really cold one that said I'd be a little late.

Morishita texted me twenty-three photos in the middle of the night. I was too scared to open them. I had decided they were all pictures of the body, so I couldn't look. What could I say when I saw him in class? Was he shocked by what I did? Did he hate me? I had no idea I could be so selfish, to just want to be left alone. I'm sorry, Morishita. I'm sorry.

"Are you going to stay home?"

My mom shook me awake. It was already morning, but I was still wrapped in my blanket. I had to leave soon, but my body wouldn't move. If I didn't go to school today, that'd be the end of everything. I couldn't move, even when I told myself that. I couldn't even come up with an excuse for my mom. I sat there silent and heard her say, "You're going to school tomorrow."

I didn't reply.

I didn't get any other texts from Morishita after that. He didn't send any message with the images. He sent me twenty-three wordless photos. That made looking at them all the more terrifying. Seeing them would tell me what he really felt. The blood in my eyes, in my heart, would probably freeze.

At about eleven, I finally got out of bed and took out my videogame system. I sat there playing, and mom called me for lunch. She scolded me for still being in my pajamas and told me to come downstairs when I was dressed. As I changed, I thought about how I was never really a good kid. I guess given that, my mom was nice. I thought about just listening to music after eating. Not idol music, but the beautiful music old men made when they were about my age. That glittering music that would stop me from seeing all the scenes appearing in my mind.

When I went downstairs to the living room, the TV was on and a news program had just started. Even now, that incident was still the top story. Suddenly, a strange boy's face filled the screen. Right as I asked, Who's this guy? my mom brought over a plate of *omurice*.

"You haven't heard? He was the first victim. You applied for

Astral Season, Beastly Season

his school, too. He's from Azayama High School. And he's even your age."

Azayama High School was close by. I had applied thinking you might wind up going there, but I didn't make the cut. It was bad luck. The test didn't go well. Afterwards, I heard you had moved to Tokyo, and I was actually relieved. You must not have made it in either. It seemed the first victim's name was Kazama Yuya. I stared at that picture. You definitely called the first victim Yu-chan. Because of that I had assumed it was a little kid, and a girl. But it was a high school junior, a boy, that you were calling Yu-chan. I stared as his face, wondering what it all meant. He wasn't as good looking as Morishita, I thought. I scooped some of my eggs and fried rice with my spoon. He's not as good looking as Morishita, not as good looking as Morishita. My *omurice* began to vanish as I thought that.

"Slow down," I heard someone say.

It seemed there hadn't been any progress in the case. That girl must not have been found yet. Had Morishita not cut her up yet? If not, then where had he hidden the body? It would be hard work carrying the body all the way from Osaki to here. Had he started to dismember her at the scene of the crime? I started to feel sick, so I changed the channel.

A weird talk show. An athlete no one cared about and an actor talking. Yeah, I'm sure you know the kind of show. But I couldn't bring myself to move away from the TV. I flipped between stupid channels, stupid shows. My mother must have been sick of it. My face spread out in front of the TV without even a hint of smile.

"Are you tired? You should lie down."

I ignored her words. I stared blankly at TV personalities and their stupid talk. Idiotic jokes, strange and intriguing factoids. My heart rattled like the lid of a kettle. This kind of world exists, too. It exists. Try to understand. Watch. What I had seen. All that I had seen. Had experienced. It was okay. That wasn't all there was. That wasn't everything in this world. In my life. Someone, somewhere was living their life trying to make all of humanity, including me, laugh. There is laughter. They try to make us laugh. I could be part of that. I could watch. I was allowed to watch. I could even laugh. Laughing was allowed. Even for me.

I was crying.

"Oh? Is that so?"

It was already evening. Hearing my mom's voice, I finally took my eyes off the TV and saw she was talking to someone on the intercom.

"Shota, a girl named Watase-san is here for you."

Mom had this surprised look on her face, but so did I.

Confused, I put on the cardigan mom handed me and tentatively opened the door. Watase was really there. She looked worried, but there she was, standing all alone. She noticed the door open just a crack and waved. I had no choice but to muster my courage and go to her. I opened the door.

"Are you all right? Did you catch a cold?"

Smiling, she handed me some printouts and photocopies of her notes.

"These are the notes of a top student. You better be grateful."

Astral Season, Beastly Season

She smiled mischievously. It was like the shining world inside the TV had crystalized, took human form, and broke out of there just for me... No. I knew I shouldn't say that. Watase came here for her own reasons, I knew that. But I could only see the world in black and white. This was white. The white which I thought only existed on TV had come here now, just for me.

"What's wrong? Are you tired?"

I was looking at the ground. Watase reached her hand out towards me. Before it touched my arm, I shook my head and smiled.

I'm fine. I'm fine.

"Really?"

I watched her fingers slide back to her side.

Yeah.

"Don't overdo it. Umm, I have to apologize for something. That's why I came."

When I looked up, Watase bit her lower lip and stared at me.

"So, the class trip's the day after tomorrow, and today we had to decide our groups."

It starts the day after tomorrow? I totally forgot about it. Where are we going again? I whispered. But it seemed Watase didn't have the time to answer.

"I'm sorry. I know it was selfish of me, but I put you in my group..."

I didn't really care. I didn't have anyone to group up with so I always wound up in whichever group needed another member anyway.

"So, the other members are Aoyama, Morishita, and this girl Taeda. Do you know her, Taeda?"

I shook my head.

"Yeah, I figured. Um, she's the one who's always with me. You know? She sits next to Morishita."

I knew who that was. She's one of his followers.

"Aoyama and Morishita are still fighting, so I kind of had to force them to be in the same group. Then Morishita said he wanted you to be in our group, too."

What?

"He said if you weren't in our group, he wouldn't join either. He probably thought that if there's another boy there, he won't have to talk to Aoyama."

Morishita had other, better male friends. I was sure of that. But it seemed that thought had never even crossed Watase's mind. She didn't seem bothered at all by the fact that Morishita named me personally.

"I'm sorry. If there's anything wrong with that, tell me. I'll get someone to trade with you. I'll arrange everything."

I nodded and said, It's fine.

Watase just gave a nervous smile. How could I show her that I really felt that? Should I just be honest and say that I wanted to be with Morishita, or really, that I wanted to be with her? Would she just think that I was bad at being sarcastic?

Watase left right away. She smiled and said she had cram school today, too.

Sorry to make you go out of your way.

"Don't worry. Today's math, and the cram school's close by so it's no problem."

Astral Season, Beastly Season

Everything she says is so gracious. Only after she shrank into the distance did I notice I should have said thank you.

The next day I went to school. As I put my phone in my bag, I remembered the photos that Morishita sent me. I wasn't particularly scared any more. On the news, they still hadn't said anything about a new body being found. I turned my phone on and opened the messages.

In those messages were the photos Morishita took of your notebook. Page to page was crammed tight with your writing. There I discovered the words "Kazama-kun" and "Yu-chan" appearing over and over. I learned that you had dated Yu-chan when you were in middle school, and that he had sent you several old photos and threatened you. I could guess from the ugly hearts you had drawn how inappropriate those photos must have been. You wrote that you decided to kill him because of that, right? In your diary. You wrote, "I'll kill him," right? But that was all a joke, right? Morishita took the pictures so I could see the notes you wrote about breaking down the body and about power spots. Have the police found this yet? Did you hide it well? All of a sudden, I was at school. I rushed to my classroom and began looking for Morishita. Assuming Morishita had seen this, that he knew now that you really killed someone, what would he do? He had already killed two people.

"Are you feeling better already?"

I turned around, and Watase was standing there. I nodded yes and then noticed something in her hand.

"This? This is our schedule for the trip. Here. This one's yours."

When I opened the booklet she gave me, I saw the names of our group members written there by hand. There we were. Me, Morishita, and Watase, and also Aoyama and Taeda.

"Oh, and let me introduce you to Tae-chan."

Watase approached a student—it must have been Taeda—and began talking to her. The moment she turned to speak to Watase, she saw me and then diverted her gaze. She clearly hated me.

"Yamashiro, Tae-chan will be in our group from tomorrow, too. Tae-chan, say something."

"Why do I have to be in a group with him? If there weren't enough people, we could have had Kazu-chan join or something."

I guess Taeda hadn't agreed to letting me into the group. Morishita still hadn't arrived.

"It was for Morishita."

"I don't get Morishita-kun either. Why would he want this guy in our group? Does he feel bad for him or something? Because he's always alone?"

"Tae-chan, you're being mean."

But Watase was laughing, too. That's right. The Watase I knew was always like that. At some point I had gotten it in my head that the Watase I had met on the train was the only Watase.

"Anyway, just don't talk to me," Taeda said, and then immediately returned to her seat. Had Watase also forgotten that just a second ago she was smiling? She followed Taeda silently. She wanted to ask Taeda something about the homework we were turning in today. *Why not ask me?* I thought.

"Good morning."

Astral Season, Beastly Season

It was that familiar voice. Morishita had arrived. He looked the same as always. Except he was talking only to me. Even though he always greeted everyone. Good morning, I answered, but I felt uneasy because Taeda started staring at us from a distance.

"What happened to you yesterday?" Morishita asked, smiling, like he hadn't the faintest intention of blaming me for anything. I couldn't respond. I couldn't tell him that I didn't come to school because I had seen him killing someone. I mean, if I told him, would he get it? I wasn't sure he would.

"We're in the same group for the class trip."

In the end, I wound up leaving school with him again.

Morning, lunchtime, and afternoon, Morishita was left alone. Aoyama and Watase didn't try to talk to him, and Taeda kept staring, but she didn't say anything either. Maybe something happened yesterday. As soon as school ended, I went to talk to Watase before I said anything to Morishita. Class had just let out, but she was already heading for cram school.

"What? Tae-chan?"

Maybe the reason everyone was avoiding Morishita was the fight two days ago, but I couldn't understand why Taeda kept watching him from a distance.

"Yesterday, Tae-chan…" Watase looked like it was hard for her to say.

Go on, you can say it, I said.

"Yeah, yesterday, she told Morishita she didn't want you in our group. Then Morishita flipped out."

Again? He did it again. I mean, he's never like that.

"I know. He was never like that before. But yesterday and

the day before, he was a bit weird. That's why I figured it'd be good to have you with us. You're the only one he's really talking to."

So you're saying I have to babysit Morishita? I couldn't actually say that. But I felt really insulted for some reason. I wanted Watase to say she wouldn't mind going on the trip with me, even if she was lying. I held myself back from telling her that she was just ditching me with Morishita so she could run off on a date with Aoyama. *I can't say that,* I thought.

"I'm sorry."

Watase sounded as though she saw right through me.

I guess the gist of things was that Morishita freaked out at Taeda, and she got scared. And because of that, she's being stupid and won't talk to Morishita. Judging from the way they were behaving, all the girls chasing after Morishita had also seen that and got worried. They were probably all wondering what happened to him, thinking he must be in a bad mood and that they should avoid saying anything wrong and just wait for him to calm down. I knew from before that the classroom was like a donut. I had always been alone in the hole in the center. Now Morishita's there. But he jumped into that hole. Ripping to shreds all the unrequited affection the girls piled on him on the way. All for you.

I could sense Morishita approaching me just as Watase edged out of the classroom. As I went to get my bag from my desk, he asked, "Going home?"

I felt like I had no right to shake my head, so I nodded instead.

"Did you catch a cold?" he asked as we left the school building and headed to the gate. When I nodded, he smiled and said, "Take care of yourself."

You didn't smile in class at all today, I thought.

Morishita, those pictures.

"Mami-chan's diary?"

Yeah.

When I saw those, I worried that Morishita's heart must have been carved up by every form of misery.

"I thought you'd want it, too. That diary."

That's all Morishita had to say.

"It's better than any merch, right? I get it, how Okayama must feel. He probably really wanted to take that home but fought the urge 'cause he figured it'd cause problems later. I wonder what Mami-chan did with it. Maybe she buried it."

Why?

"I mean, if that had been found, there's no way the police'd go so long without pressing charges. That's conclusive evidence," Morishita said.

But I didn't get it. I didn't get why he would say that. After all, if that were true, if he accepted what was written in the notebook as true, wouldn't that mean you killed someone? Wouldn't that mean you really killed Yu-chan? Wouldn't that mean we'd have to stop thinking you were innocent?

"Even if she did kill someone, I still think she's cute, and I like her, and I want to get her out of jail as fast as I can. And if she were innocent, that would mean there's another killer, and then we'd have something else to worry about."

Morishita said he was glad you were the real killer.

I didn't understand what Morishita was saying. He saw your diary. I'm sure he knew everything, that you were dating this Yu-chan guy, that he took dirty pictures of you, that you killed him for threating you with those pictures. But Morishita was smiling, and still saying that he would kill because he wanted to save you. He was hoping from the bottom of his heart to become the real killer, the one who killed Yu-chan in your place. Even though Morishita knew, knew that if he was arrested, he'd never be able to have sex with you, to kiss you. Even though he knew you'd never love him.

"It's not like I'm in love with Mami-chan," he said. "She's an idol. You can't fall in love with an idol."

I didn't understand. My legs and arms were heavy, like they'd been cut to pieces and then glued back together. I felt so sick I thought my organs would flip inside out. *Morishita, are you all right? Are you really all right? That's disgusting. What are you saying? Where are your feelings leading you? Where are they trying to take you?*

"I want to save Mami-chan as soon as I can. Let's keep going."

I didn't understand what Morishita was saying. What was he thinking? What did he think you were? When he said your name, his eyes looked like those of someone deep in worship. He even said he could kill for you. And that he wasn't in love. That you were an idol. I knew all of it, but I didn't get what he was feeling. I don't have it. That kind of feeling doesn't exist anywhere inside me. Morishita stood there like a distortion in space.

"Yu-chan was our age and a guy. I have to kill another guy soon. To get the balance right."

Morishita was looking for his next victim.

Astral Season, Beastly Season

"I've got to kill someone close to me so they can figure out I'm the killer. I wish I'd killed Okayama, then the balance would have been really good... He has my contact info, too... I would've been easy to track down."

Morishita didn't say anything about the girl he killed two days ago. I didn't want to ask, but I worked up the courage and spoke.

Morishita, what happened to that girl? It hasn't been on the news yet.

"I'm going to dump the body tonight. Tomorrow's our class trip. It's perfect. This way, I'll be in Kyoto and I won't have to worry about wanting to go check how the investigation's going."

The white soles of her feet, the soles of a dying girl held down by Morishita. I remember. I felt like an inchworm stuck to the ground. I was remembering. I don't know if that girl died after I left or if she was dead before then. I didn't want to imagine it. I didn't want to know what he was going to do with her now, either. And the guy in front of me, he didn't care about any of that at all. He was talking about who he'd kill next as if he'd already lost interest in that girl.

Morishita, weren't you planning on killing Aoyama?

"Yeah, that's the plan."

And still, I couldn't say anything about that. I couldn't say, *Stop it.* I couldn't say, *Give up on Aoyama.*

Soon after that, Morishita said goodbye like everything was normal. I guess he didn't have plans to go anywhere today. I went straight home, too.

The next day when I arrived at the school courtyard where we were supposed to meet for the trip, Aoyama was already standing at our group's designated spot. Watase and Taeda were there, too. Morishita was the only one who hadn't arrived yet.

"Good morning, Yamashiro."

Only Watase greeted me, but I wasn't in the right state of mind to respond. I could tell I was disappointed by the fact that Aoyama was still there, that he hadn't been killed. Aoyama didn't even look in my direction. We had never really talked, and I genuinely thought I wouldn't care if he died. Then Watase returned to his side. That, I didn't like.

"Good morning." Morishita had arrived. He was carrying a big bag and smiling as usual.

Right around then, someone fidgeting with their smartphone said, "It looks like someone else died." They were still talking about the power spot murders.

"Wow, Yamashiro. You didn't bring anything."

Morishita looked at my bags and laughed in astonishment. He didn't say anything to Aoyama or the others. He just squatted next to me. Did he have no intention of talking to Aoyama before we left? Was he just going to talk to me? Then I let the name Taeda slip from my mouth.

"What?"

You don't want to talk to Taeda or anything?

"I'm good. Talking to her is always irritating anyway. I prefer the quiet."

With that Morishita simply ignored the others.

Astral Season, Beastly Season

We were heading to Kyoto. We would take the bullet train to Kyoto Station. From there we would take our luggage to the Japanese-style inn we were staying at. After eating lunch, we'd all ride a bus to Kiyomizudera Temple and Kinkakuji Temple. Then we'd go back to the inn, eat, bathe, and sleep. The only thing our group mattered for was where we'd sit on the bus, and I was with Morishita the whole time. I could hear Taeda and Watase's stupid laughs, and Watase's sickly sweet voice when she talked to Aoyama. Aoyama was visibly bored.

I don't know if you've ever been to Kyoto, but I was bored, too. My parents had taken me to all those places a long time ago, and even now, I really don't get the value of that stuff. If I have to go, I'd like to go when I'm old. I most identified with the middle-aged men standing in those desolate towns I saw from the bus window. Those men walking alone, not even wearing suits. I felt both that Morishita should have just killed people like that and that I would grow up into that sort of adult. Those feelings alternated inside me as the light of the setting sun pierced my eyes.

"That was so boring," Morishita whispered loud enough for me to hear.

That's your fault. That's what you get for fighting with everyone.

Morishita didn't get what I meant. He tilted his head in confusion at my words.

"But I'm with you now. Are you always this bored?"

It seemed that Morishita was genuinely interested in how I'd answer. As he stared at me with those bright eyes of his, I thought about how he wouldn't feel anything if he saw those middle-aged men. He wouldn't even think about killing them. I'm not sure, but probably, probably Morishita doesn't know anything about what it's like to not enjoy life.

I'm always bored, I said.

"Why? If you're always bored, shouldn't you try to make your life more interesting?"

I knew what he said was correct, and precisely because I knew, I began to cry.

I couldn't tell who any of the voices I could hear from far off belonged to. Morishita's voice, too, mixed in with everyone else's, and I couldn't tell it apart from the rest.

"Seriously? He's crying."

"What are you doing? Teacher!"

"Yamashiro, what are you doing? Don't ruin the mood."

"Is Kyoto that moving? LOL."

Amidst all the noise, there was one voice that pierced my head like a needle.

"What's wrong Yamashiro? Did you get car sick?"

It was Watase. Watase. Watase was staring into my eyes. I tried to say no, that's not it. But I swallowed my words and nodded. I was carsick, that's what I wanted everyone to think.

"Teacher, Yamashiro-kun's carsick."

Watase's words signaled everyone to go silent, and the class president called our teacher.

"Are you all right?"

I nodded.

This whole commotion had obviously started when Morishita first shouted, "Hey, why are you crying?" but he didn't

Astral Season, Beastly Season

say anything to me. I'm not completely sure, but Watase probably knew I wasn't carsick. She took the barf bag from our teacher, put it in the pocket of the seat in front of mine, and then took out a handkerchief and offered it to me.

"Here. Wipe," she said softly. She knew I had cried, that I was just crying. She knew. She knew... I couldn't even thank her.

That night when we arrived back at the inn, we ate and took turns in the inn's bath. I timed my bath to make sure I wouldn't run into Morishita or Aoyama, and afterwards I sat on a bench at the bottom of the stairs and played with my smartphone. A few students walked by me, but none of them said anything. With all the students going to the bath, there must surely have been some left alone with someone else in their rooms. The idea of being left alone with someone was scary.

"Oh, Yamashiro."

Watase appeared before me, alone.

You're not going to the bath with Taeda?

"Well, Tae-chan said she had to talk to Morishita about something."

What?

"She's probably going to ask him out. It's about time every-one starts pairing up, isn't it?"

Is that okay with you? I asked without the slightest embar-rassment.

Watase just smiled.

"Is this seat taken?" she asked as she sat next to me and

opened her notebook. "If I study in our room, Tae-chan will say I'm ruining the mood."

You should just ignore her then, I wanted to say, but I knew that Watase had long been paying attention to things I neglected. When she transformed my tears into carsickness, in that moment I think I realized the acuity of her mind. Watase didn't say anything. I don't think she wanted to talk to me, so I thought I probably shouldn't distract her from her studies.

"Hm, Yamashiro?"

I'm going back to my room.

I only said that because I wanted her to talk to me, but Watase didn't try and stop me.

When I got back to the room, Morishita was sitting there by himself. He was sitting on a chair next to the window, staring outside.

Morishita, I called out to him, but he looked like he'd been thinking for a long time.

Morishita, don't kill Aoyama.

I walked up to him but couldn't make eye contact. Those words just came out, and though my muddled brain questioned why, those words must have come from my heart itself. Everything I felt was in them. That's all. While Watase was flipping through the pages of her notebook.

"Sure." Morishita didn't even ask why.

What happened with Taeda? What did he talk to her about? If he said he didn't want to go out with her, how'd he do it? There was no sign of anyone else coming back to our room. We were sharing it with boys from another group and Aoyama, but it seemed they were all in the bath. Would

Aoyama run into Watase after his bath? Would Watase tell him she liked him?

"Who should I kill?"

Of course that's what Morishita was thinking about. My throat dried out. It was just like summer. Like a desert. Was it because of the bath? I should have bought some milk. My head started to hurt like I was getting a brain freeze.

"If not Aoyama, I guess Watase's next."

Not Watase, I said.

"In that case…"

I know. How about Taeda? Wouldn't Taeda be good?

Those words came from my mouth. That's for certain. And only that was clear.

"Sure," Morishita said, looking straight at me. He didn't think anything of it. That's all I knew, but even just knowing that made me feel relieved.

My heart wouldn't stop thumping. I could see those white soles. Rows of feet were lined up, ready to stomp on everything. I chose her. I said let's kill her. I suggested it. I knew. I had to tell him right away, tell him to stop.

Sunlight came piercing through the window. People began waking up. I could hear Morishita and Aoyama. I got up slowly and went to wash my face to avoid locking eyes with them.

The afternoon of our second day we had free time. We were allowed to explore the area around Kyoto Station with our groups. We wound up going to the Philosopher's Path at Watase's request.

"Aoyama's trying to go to the University of Kyoto," Watase

told me under her breath. I knew she wanted to go to the University of Tokyo, so I didn't have to ask.

"So I wanted him to breathe the air of the neighborhood."

Aoyama didn't know that. He looked amazed at the plain Ginkakuji Temple and stuffed his face with rice dumplings. Did he even notice that we were right next to the University of Kyoto? After that, I realized Morishita hadn't talked to me at all. Or rather, Taeda was stuck to him. I was fine with being alone and used to just being a bump stuck to any group I was in. But for some reason it hurt more than usual. I guess this is what it feels like to be rejected.

"What's wrong, Yamashiro?"

Watase left Aoyama and came to talk to me several times. Every time I said I was fine, but she probably got most of what I was really feeling. She kept talking to me because she was concerned. Sometimes, Aoyama would look at me.

Shouldn't you go be with Aoyama? I would ask quietly, so he couldn't hear.

"Hmm? I'm going. But what about you?"

I'm good.

"You don't like Aoyama?"

No, that's not it. It's more that Morishita won't talk to me...

"Let Tae-chan have Morishita today. I'll hang out with you instead."

She didn't realize that I was shocked at how sudden it all was. When I made a puzzled face, she looked worried.

"Haven't you heard? Those two are dating now."

I hadn't heard. I didn't know. I didn't get it. Why, Morishita? Why?

Astral Season, Beastly Season

"So I want to let the two of them be alone today."

I couldn't hear what Watase was saying anymore. Uncharacteristically, Aoyama waved for Watase to join him. Even Watase couldn't ignore that. I just watched. Morishita and Watase and their respective couples. I just watched. That's it. I watched as myself.

That night and the following day, I actively stopped talking to both Morishita and Watase. There weren't really any group activities, and we were mostly travelling in class groups, so the timing was good. If you don't do anything, it doesn't matter whether you're on a trip or in a classroom. I watched the scenery. We entered Osaka.

Seeing the Osaka Aquarium, buying souvenirs, and even on the way home, I didn't feel any pain or loneliness sitting silently with them. I was a wooden plank. Whether Morishita or Watase noticed me or not, time rushed by and swept them along, too.

The second we arrived at school, I headed home. Without waiting for Morishita, of course. I wasn't even sure if he could see me anymore. Thinking to myself that absolutely nothing had changed, I handed my mom the *yatsuhashi* sweets I bought as a souvenir and slept like a log.

My mother's voice, footsteps, a door shutting, children's voices, and the cries of birds—another morning came smoothly crashing in, but I just kept sleeping. Today we had a day off to make up for the extra day of school from the trip.

"Breakfast is ready. Time to wake up."

Despite everything, my mom shook me awake, and when

I went downstairs there was French toast waiting for me. I watched the news as I munched breakfast. Celebrity gossip.

"They said it happened again," mom said, pouring me a glass of milk.

What?

"One of those murders. It was a kid from your class. Taeda-san?"

Information about an actress going on a date with an actor or getting divorced or something slid into my ears.

"I just got an emergency call," she said. I couldn't say anything. Maybe my mom thought that shocked me because she didn't say anything else.

I was too scared to watch the TV news, so after that I just watched old recordings. I watched some TV drama that ended last month starting from episode one. It starred the actors from the earlier gossip. And then my mom brought me lunch.

"I guess that girl wasn't the real culprit." My mom said they were talking about her being innocent on the talk shows. But I didn't want to see those shows. "I hope they catch the real killer soon."

Morishita didn't contact me.

I looked at my phone.

You didn't kill her because I said to, right? I wanted to ask him, but I didn't know what I'd do if I didn't get the answer I hoped for. I didn't know what Morishita was doing now, if he liked Taeda. What if he didn't love you, but Taeda? What if it was mutual? What if, despite that, he killed her? Because I said to? To save you? Did he hate me? Did he think I killed

Astral Season, Beastly Season

her? To Morishita, what even are you, and I, and Taeda? Do we even matter? Any of us?

"Hello?"

I called Morishita.

Can you meet me? I asked.

"Sure," he said.

We decided to meet at the small shrine by my house.

Morishita showed up wearing jeans and a T-shirt. Even though it was kind of far, he walked all the way.

"What's up?"

I heard from Watase that Taeda asked you out.

"Oh, you knew?" Morishita smiled shyly. He blushed. "It's kind of embarrassing. I mean, when we were staying in Kyoto, she said she wanted to talk to me."

And?

"So I said all right." He was smiling. Smiling, embarrassed. I couldn't say anything after that. "I didn't really mind either way, so I figured if I didn't care maybe I did like her. So I said yes. Oh, did you see the news?"

I shook my head.

"I killed her. Taeda."

It was like he was talking about a completely different person. But he said both things in the same breath.

H-huh?

"She was easy to kill." He was smiling. "Just one more," he whispered. "Just one more will be perfect. Since I cut them up and arranged them into stars, it'll make sense if I kill five people. When they catch me. Then my lawyer can say I was summoning a demon. It should be five people."

Isn't this enough? Even my mom is starting to doubt whether Mami-chan is the real killer. Isn't this enough? I wanted to say, but I couldn't speak. Taeda was dead. I said she should be next. I told Morishita to kill her instead of Aoyama or Watase. I knew that. That's all I knew. I ran away from the white soles of those feet, I ran, I ran, got on a train, but still I'm here, here listening to Morishita talk about Taeda's death. I haven't been strangled, I haven't drank any poison. But it's because of me that Taeda's dead. Even though I knew Morishita would really do it, I said Taeda's name.

Did you like her?

"Well, she was cute."

Did you like her from before she asked you out?

"I'm not sure, but I was happy when she did."

Morishita's words rattled around inside me. I opened my mouth but then swallowed. I felt like my eyes were trembling, my heart overflowing, and gaping holes were opening up all over my skin. That girl's feet had pierced my body and now they were spinning around, splitting me in two. Taeda was watching me. She was staring at me. I would break in two and spin through the sky, look down at the town, and from up there, look, the places the bodies were discovered, those power spots, from the sky, ha ha ha, they look like a star. No, they don't. Just a normal square. Look, it's like a square twisted, spinning around town. My mind, heart, lungs, stomach, back, and the precious bones and organs my mother birthed for me, are split in two and flying through the sky. Morishita, I, Morishita, I,

"Yamashiro, about the last victim… Will you kill me and cut up my body?"

Astral Season, Beastly Season

All of a sudden, Morishita went and said that.

How would you feel if someone asked you that? I'm just asking. Apparently, I didn't really listen well. Apparently, I ran my mouth and said, Please, kill me instead.

Morishita looked at me, concerned.

Listen. Morishita, if I killed you, the primary suspect would be dead, and then we wouldn't be able to save Mami-chan, I said.

"But," he said. "It'll definitely be better to be arrested than to die. You're underage. Plus, I made it so you could say you woke up some demon. I'll even put together some strange notes so you can come up with a good excuse."

Morishita was so nice. You should've dated Morishita instead of Yu-chan.

But I can't, I said, staring at Morishita. I can't, Morishita. I'm no good. I've never dismembered anyone, I said.

"I'll show you," he said. "I'll even show you how to carry the body so no one will spot you, and where to go so you'll get caught. Put these tissues with Mami-chan's DNA on them by the body," he advised.

I'm not like that, I screamed. That's hard. I can't kill anyone. I'm scared. Besides, Mami-chan really killed someone. She was the real killer. So I can't be like her. She doesn't care about me. I'm nothing more than an insect to her. She won't notice me. She'll keep on living and she won't care about me at all. I'm just a normal person. Do you get it? I'm not like Mami-chan, and I'm not like you. I'm different, Morishita.

"What? You didn't want Mami-chan to kill anyone?"

Of course, I said. It's sad, isn't it? I lived my life making fun of her. How even though she could never be a top idol, she lived so desperately, she danced and practiced like her life depended on it. I lived my life complimenting her for her hard work. But if she were a killer, if she did that, I wouldn't be able to say, Good job! You worked hard, anymore. She wouldn't be weak. Not like me...

"You mean you wanted her to keep trying, without killing anyone, to just keep trying, so you lost hope because she murdered someone?" Morishita grabbed my shoulder as he asked. He looked me in the eye. I wasn't sure what I should say.

"Yamashiro, you're fine. Stop acting all high and mighty, saying you wanted to make fun of Mami-chan. You don't have to look down on yourself. Mami-chan's a killer. You don't have to stick up for murderers. She's the bad one. You can say that you're disappointed because of that, Yamashiro."

I found myself looking into Morishita's eyes. He was staring at me. I didn't know what he thought about you, about the murder you committed. But the one thing I knew was that he was hurt. And that I was, too. I wonder if you'll understand. Morishita had never cried, but he was deeply hurt. But still, he tried to save me. I knew when he held out his hand. That hand, it was covered in blood. It was falling apart. Everything, it was for you. He didn't want to kill anyone, he couldn't, he couldn't kill anyone. But for you, because of you, he did. Because you killed. But still, but still, I like you. Even he still likes you. We will always love you, and one day, even if you have to lie, even if it takes a miracle or some sort of fluke, we want you to perform at the Budokan. We dreamed about

Astral Season, Beastly Season

it. Those of us who can't work as hard as you, who can't be as committed as you.

"You don't have to hold on to something just because you used to like it. If you're disappointed in Mami-chan, you should find some other girl. I mean, Mami-chan's just an idol in the first place. Even if you say you like her, that's a different kind of like. I mean, aren't there tons of other good girls out there?"

Morishita's voice flowed into me like cold water. It became a spring. I wanted to save that water, to keep it forever. I didn't even want to cry. But I knew, still, it would flow away.

"I got it. I won't decide who's next. I'll do what you say," Morishita spoke softly.

I like you. No matter how hard you worked, your dancing was unimpressive, your singing not that great, but still I liked you because you tried as hard as you could. You worked and worked, and I watched on, excited by how far you came. There are plenty of cute people, but you are the only one cute to me. I'm unsure if thinking you're cute, watching you work so hard, if that's a kind of condescension or not, or if I could love you, not as an idol or character, or pet, but a person. I want to be honest. Do I have the right to praise your way of life, your hard work? The right to love you? My youth was empty. Besides watching you, I had nothing. But despite that, regardless of what form it took, regardless of what you thought, how you lived, if I have given my love, all my love, to your effort, that would be enough for me. But I'm not sure if I even have love to give.

I like you. How you're just cute. The one and only, cute you. I love you. I don't know what you'll get from this, what you'll go on laughing at. I don't know if you'll be released, if you'll be found innocent, if you'll go back to being an idol, or if you'll die, suffer, be sad, if you'll just think of me as another victim, or if you'll despise Morishita. But I like you. I don't begrudge you anything. Really, I just want you to do your best as an idol, to climb the steps, and whether you fail or succeed, to say, "Well, I made it this far." I don't need your thanks. I want to say thank you for what you've done. I want to say thank you, and that I hope you think you've done at least a little good. Your smile, your effort, sweat, tears, all of that taken together, that's what makes you you. Now I can tell you. Thank you. I love you.

Morishita will bear the burden of your crime. He will turn himself in tomorrow. Probably by the time this letter gets to your mailbox, after you've been released and can read it, I'll be dead. I'll be cut up at some power spot. You probably won't think anything of that. Or maybe you'll think it's sad. Maybe you'll think I'm just a pitiful boy killed by that crazy guy, Morishita. That's fine. Don't think too hard about it. Just go on living. Long and far. I can say that because you're cute, because you're my cute idol. I won't say I died because of you. I don't hate you. You can do it. You can become a great idol. Please become an idol that someone, somewhere in the future will thank. I'm off to hell now. I'll still be cheering for you from there.

Yamashiro Shota

Astral Season, Beastly Season

The Season of Righteousness

August 14th, Sunny (Raining in Tokyo)

A long time ago, in a passage for either English or modern Japanese class, I read that at seventeen you stop being human. You stop being human and you become either a star or a beast. Now, after two years, I feel like he's become a star and that boy a beast. As for myself, even now, I have no clue at all what I've become.

There probably aren't too many people who had a classmate in their youth that turned out to be a serial killer. Most of the people I met in college take everything seriously and have experienced things like love and friendship as slightly worse versions of what's portrayed in comic books. I describe my past like they do when I talk about it. I never say anything like, "My best friend was killed by one of our classmates." Basically, I try not to ruin the mood.

"How's college?"

Burning, melting, flowing into the asphalt, slipping away, about to turn into a river. On summer days like this, my hometown feels like it's half sunk into the ocean. Today I didn't wear a cute dress. I picked out jeans and a T-shirt at random and put on just a little makeup. The boy sitting in front of me seemed a bit relieved by that.

"It's normal, I guess."

"Really? It's been so long since you've come back to visit. I figured you were having fun."

I stared at him, thinking how I'd probably never introduce him to the members of my university clubs or the people at my part-time job. The best friend of the classmate who killed my best friend. I could never say that. Oh, and I used to like him.

"What? Were you waiting for me?"

"I wasn't waiting, but still."

I thought I never wanted to see him or this town again.

"Why did you say those things?"

That is, until I read that article.

The boy sitting in front of me was Aoyama. We went to the same school all the way since elementary school. I'm not sure when he noticed that I exist, but I knew all about him. He was the sort of person you'd always see laughing at someone's jokes.

"Because I was asked," he answered.

The article. That article. That horrible article where he answered some tabloid reporter's questions. I read it last week. Serial murderer, the crazed seventeen-year-old, Boy A—no, Aoyama and I call him Morishita. Morishita, who liked green tea parfaits. Morishita, the popular kid. I knew him for a long time, too. Ever since elementary school, he was nice, popular,

Astral Season, Beastly Season

good looking. He was a fast runner and had good grades.

"Did you really have to say all that about how he was popular and good looking, that he was a fast runner and had good grades?" I screamed at Aoyama.

"I'm sorry."

"You're sorry? For what? What are you sorry for?"

"I shouldn't have done that for the victims' sake. Is that what you want me to say?"

"That's right."

"But that's not what you really think, is it? You don't care about them. You're the one who was upset by it. What you're really mad about is my attitude."

"You're wrong. That's not true."

"Yes it is."

Only now did I feel sweat beading and sliding down my cheek. I looked at him through my handkerchief as I wiped it away. He was looking straight at me. He wasn't smiling at all. And he was the sort of person who smiled both to cover up his mistakes and to condescend.

That morning I called his number from high school and thankfully got through. We agreed to meet in the afternoon. We were in a small café next to our old school. Aside from the old lady who ran the place, the two of us were the only people there. The AC was on, but the sun was still clinging to the inside of my chest. The second my burning body passed through the automatic door and I saw Aoyama sitting there alone, I wondered to myself, *Was he always so expressionless?*

"If you're pissed off, say so. You were always honest, weren't you?"

He spoke as though I had changed. And though I thought

it didn't matter if either of us had changed—what would that mean anyway?—my intentions meant nothing to him, just as his meant nothing to me.

Morishita was Aoyama's best friend since elementary school. Honestly, it was impossible for me to imagine my best friend being a murderer, and Aoyama definitely didn't understand what it felt like to have his best friend killed by a classmate. How Morishita felt was even more unfathomable. Apparently, he said he killed five people and dismembered them so some idol he liked would notice him, and when I imagine that, all I can think is that he's scum. For a few days after Morishita turned himself in, Aoyama didn't come to school. It seems he was called to the police station by the cops as he was a friend of the suspect and asked a bunch of questions, and after that, he didn't come to school for a while. According to what we later heard from the police, "Even his best friend Aoyama knew nothing about Morishita's crimes." Because no one seemed to know anything, I was also questioned by the police, just in case. I had cram school, so I arranged the questionings for Saturdays and Sundays that I didn't have practice tests for college entrance exams.

"Have you been friends with Morishita-kun for a long time?"

"Not really in elementary school. In eighth grade we were on the student council together, so we started to talk more."

"What about Yamashiro-kun?"

"What?"

I felt bad for Yamashiro. He was the last one killed by Morishita. But I was speechless for a second at the question. I was

Astral Season, Beastly Season

shocked. Tae-chan was also killed, and unlike Yamashiro, she was my close friend. If they had looked into the relationships in our class, they should have found that out right away, so why were they asking about Yamashiro first? Somehow, I managed to calmly think about all that. To me, Tae-chan's death was the most painful. That's when I noticed. I was ranking the importance of their lives. That was when I fully realized it. My eyes suddenly dried out.

"I heard that you were the one who asked Yamashiro-kun to join your group for the class trip. Was there any particular reason for that?"

"Yes. Morishita said he wanted Yamashiro to be in our group."

My heart beat sounded so close, it felt like my heart had taken the place of my brain. Twitching in the back of my ears, the vibrations of my pulse. I had to be calm and collected in front of these adults, so I exhaled deeply, closed my eyes, and quickly straightened out my thoughts.

"Were they always close?"

"I don't know. But recently Yamashiro and Morishita had been walking home from school together."

"So, you're saying the two had suddenly become friends?"

That wasn't a particularly out of character thing for Morishita to do. In my mind, Morishita was always nice to everyone, and he treated everyone the same way. So even though he was suddenly hanging out with Yamashiro, it wasn't anything stranger than like, the wind blowing from the south one day. Morishita never discriminated like I did.

But this old man would never understand that kind of

thing. "Do you know why they suddenly became friends?"

"I don't think there was any particular reason."

"That can't be the case," he said. "By the way, did you know that Morishita-kun was an idol fan?"

"No, I didn't."

"What about Yamashiro-kun?"

"I didn't really talk with Yamashiro that often."

You can tell just from looking at him that Yamashiro is an idol fan, right? Is that what he really meant? While I knew it was mean of me, I just told him that Yamashiro was gross if he was an idol fan, and if he wasn't, then whatever. How was I supposed to know what Yamashiro liked? Even though I'd known Morishita from long ago, I didn't really know anything about him.

Morishita and Aoyama fought constantly since elementary school. Or rather, Aoyama would always get mad at Morishita. In elementary school that would happen all the time because Morishita broke a promise or decided to join someone else's group for a fieldtrip without telling Aoyama. It would start with those little things that you'd expect a girl to get mad about, Aoyama would get violent, and then it would be over. But Aoyama would always break promises and Morishita always forgave him with a smile.

There was an imbalance in their dependence. We all thought that Aoyama, who relied on that twisted relationship, was definitely Morishita's best friend. Aoyama must have thought so, too. It turned out that Morishita was the only one who didn't see it that way. For some reason, I couldn't shake that thought. It was like a moist film clinging to my skin.

Astral Season, Beastly Season

"What about Morishita?"

"Him? He could be friends with anyone."

I don't know what kind of face I was making when I said that. There was no mirror there. Come to think of it, the lady who lived next to me always said that my face got really ugly when I said mean things. I could tell the detective leaned forward a bit even though I was looking down.

"What do you mean?"

"He was a good guy."

That wasn't the kind of information to spread to the mass media. No third party knew. But we, all of Morishita's classmates, we all said that when we were questioned. We all knew, even without checking with each other.

"A good guy." It seemed that we were the only ones who believed that could be an unconditionally good thing, and, apparently, it made others think, *Well, even good guys can kill people,* and made Morishita seem even more abnormal. We had no intention of making Morishita look bad. But then that officer would say, "I'd like to hear more about what you mean."

"What do you mean by 'more'?"

"What made you think he was a good guy?"

"There isn't anything in particular..."

"Is it possible it was just an act? Maybe he just had a way with words?"

It's easy to say bad things. But Morishita never said anything bad about anyone, and he never made fun of what others did. He minded his own business, and he was accepting of everyone. But you could also call that kind of attitude cold or disinterested.

"So he was indifferent to his classmates?"

"No, that's not right."

"Really?"

There was no point in being stubborn. Who was I trying to cover for? Morishita killed Tae-chan. He killed Yamashiro. I shouldn't worry about throwing stones. It doesn't matter how nice he was to me. I should forget about how after I failed a test, when I was depressed, he treated me to a parfait on the way home. I should just say it was all a performance. Everyone wanted me to. I was sure even Morishita didn't care what I said.

You become either a star or a beast. When you turn seventeen. I recalled those words I read somewhere in my studies. Here I was, like a spectator, watching myself desperately try to become neither a star nor a beast but a human. If what I was trying to protect was "humanity," did that, in the end, amount to nothing more than narcissism?

"No, I don't know. Maybe some parts of it seemed fake."

"I see." The detective nodded, just a bit self-satisfied. Morishita wouldn't have killed anyone if he was a good guy. Even I understood that much. It's because he wasn't a good guy that he killed people. That was the best way to think about it. In order to keep breathing, tomorrow, and the day after that.

"Aoyama, when the police called you in, did you tell them the same thing?" He looked at me suspiciously for acting as though I forgot how uncomfortable we were just a second ago.

Astral Season, Beastly Season

"What?"

"They questioned you, right?"

"Yeah."

"Did you talk about Morishita like you did in the magazine?"

"Yes."

I took the magazine out of my bag. On the cover were big letters reading, "The Bizarre Murders and Surprising Past of Boy A," and Morishita's handsome face with a black bar across the eyes. We knew the big, beautiful eyes behind there. We had been reflected in those eyes.

"You brought that?"

Aoyama looked a little upset. I ignored him and opened the magazine. The article Aoyama was interviewed for was a special feature wherein Friend B details the past of Boy A. A dispassionate description of Morishita's life in elementary, middle, and high school.

"Is this all true?"

"You should know. It's real."

"I didn't talk to Morishita that much when we were young, so I didn't really know him then. Did you exaggerate anything?"

"I mean, they embellished a little."

According to Friend B, Boy A had been popular since elementary school. Girls liked him, and boys flocked to him. Before class trips, for example, classmates would always argue over whose group he would join. Because Boy A would never express his own preference, this often led to conflicts.

"Boy A also had a habit of giving his things to others.

Friend B said that because he'd even try to give away expensive things like video games, Friend B often had to stop him... Is this true?"

"It's true. You probably got things from him, too. Books, pencils."

"Yeah, if you borrowed an eraser, he'd say you can have it. Everyone else took them, but I always gave them back."

"Giving stuff back to him started to be a pain. He didn't have any bad intentions or anything, so every time I'd refuse to keep something, he'd get depressed."

"Yeah, he was like that. Wait. But Aoyama, you always refused to take his stuff, too, didn't you?"

Aoyama's eyes opened wide at my words.

"What? You knew?"

"Yeah."

The first time I noticed Aoyama was in elementary school when Morishita was giving the other boys some type of pencil that was popular back then. Out of them all, only Aoyama snuck the pencil he received back into Morishita's desk. When he returned to his seat, Morishita immediately discovered the pencil and cocked his head in confusion. Who returned that pencil and why? Morishita probably didn't know.

"When I saw that I thought, 'Wow, Aoyama's a good guy.'"

Aoyama shifted his eyes away from me and took a sip of his ice coffee.

"Anyway, I told the police about how he'd give things away, too. But they just thought he was handing things out to get people to like him. I couldn't stand that."

Aoyama drew an arc with his fingers.

Astral Season, Beastly Season

"I see... So that's why you told someone else?"

"How can I put this? Morishita was the kind of guy who thought it was normal to do things for others. He wasn't thinking about acting morally, he just thought doing those things was normal, and he didn't think he was losing out on anything. Even those pencils, he just thought that if everyone else was happy, he didn't need any. He bought them himself, you know? With his allowance. But, well, once we were in middle school no one really tried to take anything from him, and the ones who actually did were all kind of weird."

"Yeah."

Aoyama nodded like he had made up his mind. "Morishita isn't a bad guy."

"But he killed people."

"That's right."

"Five people."

"That's right." Aoyama covered his head in his hands and looked down.

Aoyama and I aren't stupid, we aren't Morishita's parents, and we don't believe he's innocent. I mean, he turned himself in. And now he's in a jail cell.

"It wasn't right."

Aoyama was silent.

"When the families see that article, they'll be hurt," I said. "Aoyama, it's already been two years."

I realized those words didn't mean anything to Aoyama. His hands covered his eyes. Those same hands then pulled hard at his hair. And then Aoyama let out a deep groan.

"You're so cold."

"What?"

"How could you just apply to college? How could you get in?"

Aoyama started talking fast. And then, suddenly, I remembered I used to like him.

"Normally when this kind of thing happens, you can't study, and you definitely can't just take entrance exams."

"But the exams weren't going to wait for me."

"But…" I could see the arteries on the back of Aoyama's hands. They bulged, vanished, and then reappeared even more clearly. It looked like he was breathing through them. "You're so cold."

He spoke as though his words were justice. I couldn't stop blinking, so I took a deep breath without making a sound. *I don't get you. What are you saying all of a sudden?* It would be easy to say that, but, on the other hand, I got a sort of rough gist of what he wanted to tell me.

"Aoyama?" I called his name, intending to set him straight. But he didn't stop.

"You're the worst. The worst, Watase."

"Aoyama, whether you're right or not has nothing to do with me. It doesn't matter which of us is right. Just because you're correct doesn't mean you have the right to hurt someone. That's all I know. You hurt me, and if that makes the pain, the burden of college entrance exams, and the fact that you still haven't gone to college go away, then that's fine. But you shouldn't be dragging righteousness into this. You shouldn't be trying to force the responsibility for the emptiness you hate so much onto me either. It's not the place for you to be

Astral Season, Beastly Season

justifying your own violence. Righteousness has absolutely nothing to do with violence."

"..."

"They're unrelated. As long as you're concerned with whether you're right or not, we can't discuss anything."

Aoyama looked at my face and spat out in a whisper, "Look, you always cry."

Something hot, but a different temperature from the summer, ran down my cheek and fell to the table. I could hear Aoyama sigh. He didn't get it. Aoyama didn't get anything. I wasn't shaken up. I wasn't scared. It's just that that was the only way. There was no other way to make him see how I felt. The only other choice I had was to throw my glass of ice water in his face and run. And the only reason I didn't do that was my pride.

"Watase."

I won't become like you, I thought as I stared at Aoyama. He finally looked straight into my eyes. I let out a long sigh before speaking.

"Yes?"

"Do you still like me?"

He spoke as though the invisible breath he let out was black.

"What?"

"Didn't you give me presents on Valentine's Day before?" He moved his fingers. Right before my eyes, he started counting on his fingers.

"So what?"

"I wouldn't mind going out with you."

"What?"

I had thought I liked this person. And I guess I still did even now. We had plenty of classmates who thought Aoyama was pitiful for chasing after Morishita and never meaning anything to him, who thought that without Morishita he wasn't anything. I hate people who can't do anything but rank others like that, but I also realized there was nothing we could do about them, it's just a part of our immaturity. Aoyama never noticed them. He would never consider making fun of others to relieve his own stress, and he could never even imagine someone saying that he just hung out with Morishita to improve his own standing. That's why I could never hate Aoyama.

"There's no way."

That's why I said it. Why I answered that way. I felt like my heart flipped upside down, turned inside out, that my blood was spurting from my body and falling to the white floor, that I had vanished. My empty, dried-out organs gurgled and swayed on the chair. That was my heart's attempt at beating. My best attempt at living. That's how it felt. Now. I have to. I have to dump my water on Aoyama.

"Huh? Why?"

Aoyama blinked and looked at me strangely.

"So you hate me now?"

"That's not it."

"Really? Well, why then?"

What? Do you really think you're going to get me to say something like, *It's not like you like me*? Bastard.

Astral Season, Beastly Season

Occasionally these white gusts of wind will pass in front of me. They're the little sandstorms that happen so often in summer here. After going to Tokyo, I eventually stopped seeing them. My friends born in Tokyo said they'd never heard of them, but still, I saw them all the time when I first moved there. They were probably hallucinations. Even now, I regularly dream about things like forgetting that it was my turn to clean the classroom and going home without doing my job.

In my hand was an empty glass.

Drops of water trickled from my fingers like miniature rain and spread over the table. In front of me, Aoyama was wiping his face with a towel he borrowed from the old shopkeeper.

He didn't say anything.

Why didn't I run away? I was definitely the one who dumped the water on him. Aoyama was silent. I had to say something. Should I apologize? But then I shouldn't have thrown the water in the first place. Why did I put myself in such an annoying situation?

Suddenly, everything became annoying.

Why did I come here? Why did I decide to meet Aoyama after all this time? I should have just ignored the magazine. It wasn't just because I thought it was bad for the relatives of the dead. Was it curiosity or something?

"What was that?" Aoyama didn't wait for me to speak.

"Why aren't you angry?"

"Did you want to make me angry?"

He was strangely calm. Seeing that relieved me. Maybe I

didn't run away because I wanted to see him calm. What a selfish thing to hope for.

"I figured I'd rush home after you freaked out."

I kept letting all these things I didn't even think slip out. Well, actually, that was probably what I really thought.

"What?"

"I came to talk about Morishita. And that magazine. Okay? Not whether we'd go out or not. It was weird to say that. You knew it was weird, didn't you? And that's why you're not angry, right?"

"Yeah, I know."

"Wow, you acknowledged that right away."

"Also, all I have to dump on you is this ice coffee, so…"

Aoyama pointed at his coffee with a half-smile. "Apparently you can't get coffee stains out, so you know…"

"Right."

"Watase, did you really come all the way here just because you were worried about the families of everyone who died?"

He took his eyes off me before he dropped those lines. He dragged his finger through the water on the table, making a straight, horizontal line that divided our respective territories.

"Yeah."

"I won't deny that it'll upset them. That's true. But, I… I thought it was cold of you. When I heard you got into college…"

"…"

"I couldn't go on without thinking about it. About how if you weren't so cold, then you'd give me a look or something to show that you like me. Do you get me?"

Astral Season, Beastly Season

"Aoyama?"

"I didn't get in. I didn't pass the first or second round of tests. I wasn't even close. Even now, I'm nowhere near good enough to get in. Most of our classmates left because of what happened. Our teachers all quit, saying they had to take care of their families or something, and all my mom cares about is my little brother's middle school entrance exams."

The shopkeeper came with a rag to wipe up the water on the table. I choked down my words, and Aoyama kept talking.

"I should've gone to Keio. I got in. It was some weird department, and private university is expensive, but I should've gone. But I rejected them, and now I'm still here. My mom wanted me to go. She couldn't waste money on more cram school to help me prepare for tests. Iwai sent a letter with a picture of him scuba diving. I saw that and thought about everything up till last year and realized there's no way I can make it."

He raised his eyebrows sharply and looked at my face. For some reason I remembered him as a child. Back when he'd punch Morishita all the time.

"If you got in, you wouldn't go out with me, would you?"

For some reason, I smiled at him.

"Yeah." He nodded awkwardly. I felt the flesh of my cheeks pull back into an awkward smile.

"Would that be more convenient for you? If I just sat here and took it while you criticized me for going off to college? If I were still the same girl in high school who liked you? Would that be convenient for you and your life as a college reject? Do you want me to be your punching bag? Is that what you think of me? That I'm a punching bag?"

"But you…"

The line of water no longer remained on the table. Aoyama was looking at me. "I was hurt when I saw this article. I was sad. Tae-chan died." My confession came out like I was coughing up the air in my lungs, coughing up my organs.

Aoyama was silent. And then I hit the magazine lying on the table. The paper was wet and stuck to my palm.

"You said I came because I was pissed off. You're right. I don't care about how the families feel. I was fed up, because even though it's only been two years, someone already popped up to defend Morishita. You know what? I want to be interviewed, too. The information I have is all worthless, and no one would want to listen, but I want to be interviewed. I want to talk, to cry. I want to scream at Morishita, 'Why did you kill Tae-chan?' I want to scream at you, too. Maybe you don't know, and maybe Tae-chan and I weren't friends since elementary school, but we were close. We shared plenty of secrets. She seriously said she wanted to marry Morishita. I half made fun of her, but I was half jealous, too. I said, 'Wow, you sure have high hopes for your unrequited love.' Her fingers were so thin, I was jealous. When I said I wanted fingers like hers, she said her legs weren't long like mine. But you don't care about that kind of talk, do you? It's not important, is it? But I want someone to listen to me talk about it. I want to ask what's real. It's not sad, painful, crushing. Compared to what Tae-chan suffered, it's not any of those things. There are no words that can show how I feel. So I can't shout my truth, Aoyama."

"I…" And that's when Aoyama's phone rang.

"Pick it up," I said without waiting for Aoyama's reaction.

Astral Season, Beastly Season

"But I don't know this number."

"Pick it up."

Aoyama silently pressed ACCEPT CALL.

"Hello… What? … Excuse me? Yes, that's me. How did you know? What? Now? All right. How can I recognize you? Okay."

And then he hung up.

"What was that?"

"One of the victims' relatives."

"What?"

"He said he saw the article."

"Huh."

"I'm sorry…" he muttered. "I'm sorry about the article, and I'm sorry for the whole going out thing."

I didn't say anything. I just gave a slight nod.

Aoyama said whoever he talked to on the phone was in town. "He said to go to our old school. I'm sorry. I gotta go."

"I'm going, too."

"Why?"

"I'm worried."

No matter how you look at it, that article praising Morishita must have made all the victims' relatives unhappy. Aoyama could have been walking off to get beat up.

"You can come along if you want, but I don't know what's gonna happen." Aoyama picked up our check.

"Aoyama," I said, taking out my wallet and handing him the cash for my drink.

"Hey, umm…" Aoyama tried to say something, but I walked out of the café before he finished.

The shadow of the eaves covered just my eyes, like the

shadow of the straw hats I was forced to wear when I was young. The sound of the stinging heat rang through some unknown part of me, maybe my skin or my eardrum. Aoyama came out after me. His face twisted at the heat, like he crashed into something solid. I placed my hand against my forehead to block the sun and stepped out onto the burning asphalt.

"It's been forever since I've gone back to the school."

"It's summer vacation so no one'll be there."

Aoyama was wearing a collared shirt—something I'd never seen in high school—and he looked more adult. There were no holes in his jeans, either.

"You don't ever go to school? It's so close."

"I don't have that kind of time." Aoyama rebutted sharply, a faint smile still on his lips.

As we started climbing the hill to the school gates, we saw several kids who looked like students coming down on their bikes. They shot us passing glances and went on their way. No one was wearing uniforms, because if they were coming to school, it was just for club activities. It didn't seem like they paid any attention to us.

"This is the first time I've ever walked up this hill," Aoyama said.

"I always walked."

"It's hard on a bike, too, you know."

"Yeah, it is steep."

Aoyama's shirt was completely dry. He might have even forgotten I had dumped that glass of water on him.

Astral Season, Beastly Season

When we got close to the gate, we saw someone sitting by the side of the road. I could see his boney shoulders even through his green T-shirt. The skinny man was facing away from us.

"Excuse me." Aoyama spoke without hesitation.

"So you're Aoyama?"

He stood his long body up and looked straight at Aoyama. His face was sunken, and eyes spread wide.

"Yes."

"Nice to meet you. I'm Okayama, from the phone."

Okayama. That was the name of the third victim.

"And who's this?"

Okayama pointed straight at me.

"Umm, she's…"

"Is this your girlfriend?"

"No. She was a classmate. We've just been talking."

"Oh, so she knows all about the incident."

"I wouldn't say that."

Okayama clicked his tongue at my reply but didn't say anything in return. He looked up the hill and stretched.

"So, this is your school?"

"Yes," I answered in Aoyama's place.

"Can we get into the classrooms? Like the one you were in back at the time of the murders."

"It's summer vacation so that would probably be difficult."

"Hey, do you know why I'm here meeting this guy?" Okayama spoke in a single breath as he continued to look up at the school. I knew he was talking to me because of the question. But he didn't look at me.

"I know."

"Did you see the magazine? What did you think?"

"I thought that it was not a very good thing to do."

"Really?" Okayama turned to look at me as if to mock me. "Why? How can someone who's not even involved feel that way? Please, give me the details. Aoyama, he was just sharing his memories of his old friend, right? Why would you think that's bad? Who do you even think you are?"

His big eyes. Meaningless question marks, his eyes on me, I didn't have any options. I knew my eyes, my eyes were widening like they were being drawn open by him. I could only breathe through my mouth, and the roof was dry and it hurt. Tightening, someone deep in my throat, someone like me screaming that they're about to get washed away. Caught, my throat, the back of it so hot like it was caught on something. Suddenly someone was pulling on my shoulder.

"Watase really came to tell me that I shouldn't have done that interview. She's not saying that because of you."

It was Aoyama's voice. It was Aoyama holding on to my shoulder.

Aoyama was looking at Okayama, not me.

"What?"

"She doesn't have any bad intentions."

"Even if she didn't mean anything bad, she should apologize if she offended me."

"For what?"

"I'm saying people who aren't involved shouldn't be butting their heads in."

"Is that really what you think?"

Astral Season, Beastly Season

"What? You again? Don't take that attitude with me."

"Aoyama!" Confused, I covered Aoyama's mouth with my hand.

"I'm sorry. I know I've been speaking out of place. And you're right, I'm not involved. I'm sorry."

"Yeah, right."

Okayama calmed down fast. And his face tensed up. Maybe that was him trying to smile.

"I tried to go into the school earlier, but a security guard stopped me. It's too bad. I came all the way here. Are there any cafés or something around here?"

Okayama started walking away from the school.

"If you wanted to go to a café or something, you should've come to where we were."

"Huh?" Okayama scrunched his eyebrows at Aoyama's words, but Aoyama ignored him.

"Excuse me, but Okayama-san, what exactly is your connection?"

"I'm her brother. My little sister was killed. You know the one. The third victim."

That was surprising. I had seen that girl on the talk shows. She was probably still in middle school. She had puffy cheeks and was very cute. But she was related to this guy.

"I was living alone in Tokyo, and my sister said she wanted to get scouted in Harajuku. She was only staying with me for three days."

"And that was when…"

"I don't know what she was doing going out in the middle of the night, but somehow she was kidnapped by Morishita. I told her Tokyo was dangerous and not to go wandering around outside."

But it was Morishita's fault. I know it's obvious, but that's what I thought in that moment. I grew incredibly embarrassed for having thought that.

"Were you close?"

"Not at all. She was grossed out by staying with me, and I didn't get what she was thinking at all either."

After a pause, he continued. "But I didn't want her to die. And I can't believe the murderer was a fan of the same idol as me."

"What?"

"I knew Morishita, too. He was following this underground idol, and sometimes he'd come to shows. I always wondered why someone with a face like his was into idols."

"… You mean she's not famous? What exactly is an underground idol?" asked Aoyama.

"What? You don't know?"

Okayama looked mockingly at Aoyama's surprised face.

"You were best friends, but you don't even know about his favorite underground idol? She's the one who was first suspected in this case. Her name's Aino Mami. She was cute, but she partied a little too hard and ruined herself."

"I've never heard of her."

"So you don't know about the first victim? Morishita must have stolen Mami-chan's diary. That's why he killed him."

"Her diary?"

"I saw him. He would sneak backstage during concerts.

Astral Season, Beastly Season

He must have been stealing Mami-chan's things. She always carried her diary with her. I think he must have secretly read that. I mean, I did it, too… But the first victim, he was Mami-chan's ex."

"Oh, him," said Aoyama.

"What, you knew him?"

"Not really. We went to the same cram school."

Aoyama crossed his arms and tilted his head. He must have been trying to remember something.

"Tell me, did Morishita go there too?"

"He did in our sophomore year. And yeah, when Morishita heard that guy was from Azayama High School, he went to talk to him. So that guy was dating an idol? He looked pretty average."

"So you're saying Morishita got jealous and killed him?" I butted in to ask. Online, people were saying that he killed people to cast some kind of black magic spell to make an idol fall in love with him.

"Apparently Mami-chan hated her ex. Morishita must have found that out from her diary and decided to kill him for her… And when I think about how Minori got caught up in all that… It's just the worst."

"Hey, Watase." Aoyama said to me. "We just left that café, so it would be a bit awkward if we went back. Should we go to the shrine over there?"

"The shrine? But…"

"Let's go."

That shrine, that was where Yamashiro's body was found.

Did Aoyama and Okayama not know what that place was? Yamashiro was found dead by the big tree at the back of that shrine. Because it was at the back, if you just went thinking it was a normal shrine, you wouldn't notice the bouquets of flowers left there for him. I had been to that place countless times, but there were never many flowers, which irritated me, but I also knew there was no reason to be irritated. Thinking about it exhausted me. My classmates said it's easier to not think about it—the ones with vivid imaginations wound up taking time off school.

It's fine. Even if everyone forgets Tae-chan. If they forget Yamashiro. If they act like Morishita never existed. That's just a way to get through it. No one has the right to criticize them for doing that. Still, I wanted to be someone's accomplice. I wanted someone to say there's nothing we can do about it. I wanted to ask someone, "It's not wrong to smile like normal at how delicious your food is, right?" To live, to be alive, and to still be happy. High school juniors, seniors, nodded at each other approvingly. They wanted to live their youths. But Aoyama, he was different. From the very beginning, he protested removing Morishita and Tae-chan and Yamashiro's desks from the class, and even when we moved up a grade, those three empty seats remained. In particular, no one could understand the reasoning for keeping Morishita's seat, and no matter what Aoyama said, no one cried over his absence. "Look at reality," they said. "Even Aoyama hit that kid." Aoyama always used to be the center of our class. In truth, it was Morishita who was in the center, but everyone knew that Aoyama was always by his side, so he, too, was always there like a central figure. But still. Those days no one talked to Aoyama.

I knew. Everyone was trying to erase Aoyama from their minds along with the dead and the criminals. So they could go on living. There are things you can't look at if you want to keep living. It's only natural that you must avoid those people who try to keep looking directly at the things we must not acknowledge. And as everyone else hunkered down and started studying for college entrance exams, I watched Aoyama.

I may be the most cowardly person involved in all this. Even as I watched Aoyama, I tried to forget Morishita. And Tae-chan and Yamashiro, too. There were times I'd suddenly feel so sick I'd puke, but still, I made time to laugh with my friends. I went to Christmas parties. I exchanged birthday presents. That's right. We turned eighteen and told each other things like, "We're real friends, right?" I felt like that was completely idiotic, but I also couldn't help thinking that in terms of my life this time was supposed to be like a festival, so I had to enjoy it. You study hard for entrance exams, so that's what I did. That's all. But I knew Aoyama was watching us with resentment.

"That's where Yamashiro died. You know, right?" I asked.

"I know." Aoyama looked at me like he was shocked. He must have seen my miserable face. When I looked into his eyes, that's when I realized. Aoyama wasn't bothered by it. He was fine going to the place Yamashiro was killed. Yamashiro's death was just a matter of fact to him.

"Should we get some flowers? It's been a long time since I've been."

I had to work up the courage to say that, but Aoyama dismissed it and quickly walked on. "Yamashiro didn't care about flowers."

"What's with this guy? Does he even think what he did was wrong?" Okayama grumbled as he rushed behind Aoyama.

"I don't think he does," I said.

"Is that even possible?"

"Aoyama really thinks all he did was share some memories of his friend."

"There was no reason to do that so publicly."

"That's true…"

"Morishita never did anything to you?" Suddenly Okayama was staring into my face.

"Excuse me?"

"Were you almost killed or something?"

"No."

"What about your friends? Were they all right?"

It was much later that I noticed a hole had painlessly opened up in the middle of my heart, as though my body were trying to split itself apart.

Though the police and the media once used to stake out the shrine, now it was silent besides the winding of the wind and the occasional whisper of grass. We climbed the stone steps, Okayama stopping frequently to catch his breath. We'd wait a bit for him, and then when he started climbing again, we'd follow along. It was so hot it felt like I was carrying a flame on my back.

"If one of your family members was killed by Morishita,

would you still say the same things?" Okayama asked Aoyama as we climbed.

"I don't know. I can't even imagine that."

"Imagine it, even if you can't picture it perfectly. How does it feel?"

With each step, one of them would let another verbal punch fly, but they never looked at each other. They just glared at the stone steps.

"Was Morishita really like the person you described in the article?"

"He was a good guy. Apart from being a murderer."

"So he was a freak who passed as a good guy. Apparently it's hard to spot the really bad guys."

"If that were true, I would have noticed. I knew him from elementary school. He was a good guy."

"He had probably just been tricking you the whole time. It could be like an instinct for him. He's probably just the dangerous type."

It had been a long time since I'd heard anyone talk about Morishita. And that wasn't because I left for Tokyo. I was sure there wasn't anyone who wanted to talk about him in this town either. Aside from Aoyama. And still, those two people in front of me discussing him, they never said anything like, "I wonder how he is now." Shouldn't we ground our own lives in what kind of person he is rather than what kind of person he was?

That's all I care about.

"Who cares about all that?" I found myself muttering at how stupid it all was.

In that moment Aoyama turned and glared at me with a face like I'd never seen before. "What did you say?" The instant he spoke, I sensed his leg flying at me, so I stepped back. It was my own fault that I missed the step. Aoyama may have tried to kick me, but he stopped himself. Still, my body was afloat. I felt like the earth was trying clumsily to shove me away from itself. While my body moved, I had left my heart behind. That moment, I couldn't speak, and then, Okayama grabbed my arm.

"Are you all right?"

His fingers were thin but rough.

"Thank you."

Maybe it was because my skin was dry. A scratching sensation enveloped my wrist.

"Watase, what do you mean who cares?"

I didn't respond to Aoyama.

"I'm sorry I made you unhappy. But am I forbidden from thinking these things? Isn't that hypocritical?"

Aoyama was calm. Okayama held on to my arm in silence.

"All Morishita did was kill people," Aoyama said.

Tae-chan died. That was Morishita's fault. That's all. It's not our job to evaluate Morishita's standing as a human. That would be meaningless.

"Morishita did nice things for you too, all the time."

"Yeah, Morishita was nice to me, and he killed Tae-chan. That's all we can say about him, Aoyama. I don't care whether he's a good guy or not. What's the point of proving that he is? Even if we conclude that he is a good guy, he won't be happy about that."

Astral Season, Beastly Season

"But we could protect his honor."

Aoyama was desperate, but it seemed to me he wasn't just speaking out of his attachment to Morishita.

"I don't know. If Morishita wanted to protect his honor, I don't think he would have done something like this in the first place."

"What are you saying?"

"You want to make Morishita into a good guy for your own sake. That's all. Just stop it already."

I gave a faint smile as I said that. After almost being kicked, some things just didn't matter anymore. Maybe that was the first time I had been truly angry at Aoyama. It just felt like, *What?* I couldn't tell if the face Aoyama was making was angry or sad. Okayama was next to me pulling at his hair. I could hear the sound of Aoyama taking a long breath. And then, "So we should just say he's a serial killer? So that anyone, even those who have nothing to do with him, can discriminate against his sister and parents, even beat them up, and then think to themselves, *Well, they probably deserve it.* I bet you don't know. You went to Tokyo, so you don't know. Morishita's sister, she started getting bullied at school. She couldn't even speak anymore, so she moved somewhere. His mom, she killed herself. His dad still lives here. People throw rocks through his windows, and one day they even tried to set his house on fire. Everyone thinks that's just how it should be. That it's their own fault for giving birth to that awful serial killer. No one even thinks of Morishita as a human anymore. Some people are terrified of him 'cause he's so unhuman, and the same number look down on him for that. There isn't anyone who tries to see him as he really is. If he did even just a tiny good deed, they assume there must be some sort of ulterior motive behind it. Even the people he's always been nice to just say, 'Wow I could've been killed. How crazy is that? He gave me a pencil one time. I could've been next.'

"Why do they get to say those things? Morishita hung out with everyone, didn't he? We ate green tea parfaits together. Didn't you eat the *mochi* balls he gave you from his parfait? Why does everyone forget these things? He gave those to you because you were upset, and you like them. Why did you forget? Do you think it's something you can just forget?"

"I haven't forgotten."

"But…"

"I remember that. And I remember that he killed people. That's all I know about Morishita."

Aoyama was silent.

"Have you met with his father?"

"I haven't seen him in a long time. I can't."

"What about his sister? You two were close, weren't you? You used to play with her."

"I can't see her. She moved to some town where no one knows about what happened. She might have even moved overseas."

"Why don't you try to contact any of them?"

"Because they'll get upset."

Aoyama closed his eyes softly. A tear ran down his cheek like a straight ray of light descending from the sky. I watched it fall.

"They didn't want to see you?"

"I don't want to talk about it anymore."

Astral Season, Beastly Season

"Yeah, that's enough," said Okayama. He was smiling. And still holding on to my arm. He pulled me hard towards himself.

"Okayama-san…"

"Morishita was your classmate?"

Okayama ignored me. I was worried about Aoyama since he was crying, so I tried to look his way, but then I suddenly realized Okayama's grip was too strong. It hurt. My wrist. Even though my face twisted in pain, Okayama didn't let up. For some reason he was staring at me, so I answered his question.

"We were in the same group for our class trip. My best friend liked Morishita, and they started going out the day before he killed her."

"I wonder if he started dating her to kill her."

"I'm not sure." Suddenly his grip tightened. "That hurts!"

I looked up and saw Okayama smiling. Popular, but a murderer. That's actually quite a common pattern. Even I've seen that on TV, Okayama-san.

"Um, excuse me."

"What?"

I felt like vomit was lodged in my throat. It was hard to breathe, but I moved my sticky tongue and said, "My arm." It looked like Aoyama hadn't noticed my pain. At some point, he had wiped away his tears and started climbing again.

"Oh, I'm sorry."

Okayama carefully released my arm. But my wrist was red. Okayama turned his back to me and followed after Aoyama as though nothing had happened.

"So your best friend was that Taeda person?"

"That's right."

I guess he planned to keep asking questions.

"She liked Morishita?"

"It seemed like it."

I heard someone click their tongue. The sound came from Okayama's direction. "She had no sense."

"Right."

"And what do you mean, 'they started dating'? Who asked who out?"

"Oh, she asked him."

As we got further up the stairs, the breeze grew stronger. My hair fluttered in the wind, and the sweat on my skin began to evaporate. But after the cool sensation passed, I sank back into the heat. Neither of them seemed to notice. I rubbed the red part of my wrist with my fingers.

"Really? Why did he say yes? He's an idol fan. And he was in the middle of his murder spree for Mami-chan."

"I really don't know."

It's true that if he had really planned to kill Tae-chan, you could say he agreed to go out with her in order to kill her.

"If that's the case he's a real monster. Hey, Aoyama, what do you think? Are you listening?" Okayama seemed to think it was funny because he laughed as he asked. "I said what do you think?"

When Aoyama failed to respond, Okayama continued. "Whether he said yes to kill her or decided to kill her after he said yes, he's awful either way."

Okayama snapped his fingers. Aoyama asked expressionlessly, "Couldn't that have all been a coincidence?"

Astral Season, Beastly Season

"Doesn't that seem pretty unlikely?"

"But…"

"He killed people, you realize? You know what that means, right? What are you defending him for? Morishita's a murderer. He's a lowlife. You get it, right?"

"Please stop"

I rushed to get between them. I stared into Aoyama's face. The blood had drained from it. It looked so lifeless it was almost scary to think that Okayama was looking at him while he pressed him endlessly for answers.

"What?" responded Okayama.

"Can we just walk?" I said.

"But I want him to understand."

"Can't you just accept that some people don't get these things?"

I pulled on Aoyama's hand and rushed up the rest of the steps, as if to run from Okayama.

When we made it to the top, there in front of us was a simple shrine. As Aoyama and I walked over to pray, Okayama stayed back alone looking up at the shrine building.

"What's wrong?"

By the time I returned, Okayama seemed to have calmed down. He exhaled.

"I was wondering what it feels like to kill someone here."

"What?"

"Did he bow in front of the shrine before he did it?"

Okayama's eyes suddenly flung open. It was the same face he was making when we first met.

"Morishita killed so Mami-chan would like him. He killed in her place, and he will never tell anyone that's why he did it. He did it all so she would love him. Did he pray for that? Here. To reach his goal he even killed someone who actually liked him… He's so heinous. He's disgusting. I get so mad when I think my sister was killed for something as pathetic as that…"

Aoyama and I had no words to respond.

"That's why I'm going to expose Morishita for what he really is. When she hears that he killed someone who liked him, I'm sure even Mami-chan will be disappointed in him."

I didn't understand how Okayama felt. It's possible even he didn't understand. I didn't sense any attachment in his words, not even to the name "Mami-chan." Did he really want to show her what Morishita really is? I couldn't completely believe that. He was just repeating the name of that idol to drown out some other voice. I didn't know him well enough to say for sure that the other voice was one of panic.

What was Aoyama thinking now? It didn't matter. I've never been able to understand his real feelings. All I knew was that no one was right, and no one was wrong, and none of that even mattered. Okayama took a long, shallow breath.

It had been two years, but there were still flowers in the spot where Yamashiro had been found. Okayama sat there silently. He pulled a picture out of his wallet and placed it in front of himself. It was a picture of a cute girl singing.

"Who's that?"

"This is Mami-chan. Yamashiro was also one of her fans."

"What? Really?"

Astral Season, Beastly Season

Okayama looked up at us and seemed shocked at our surprise.

"You guys didn't really know him?"

"I didn't," Aoyama answered plainly.

"But he was in our group for our class trip," I added hastily. Did I say that because it felt like Yamashiro was here with us? Why was I panicked?

"He was in our group, but I hardly talked to him," Aoyama said.

"I talked to him a few times."

Why did Okayama want to know about this too?

"What kind of guy was he?"

"He was a bit dark, but there was nothing bad about him," I answered.

"Huh? You mean you didn't really know him?" As he said that, Okayama brought his palms together gently. "I saw Yamashiro at a lot of concerts. He was never with Morishita, so I never imagined they went to the same high school."

Okayama stood up and looked down at the picture he had just placed there. This idol called Mami-chan. Her thin body was wrapped in pink.

"W-wait. That means that Morishita killed Yamashiro, another fan, for this idol that he liked?"

"Maybe he agreed to be killed."

"What? What does that even mean?"

"It's just something I imagined."

Okayama pulled a black notebook out of his bulging jean's pocket and began writing something down. When I looked, he was writing the name, "Yu-chan," and, "Same cram school

Morishita sophomore year, seen talking by Aoyama. Ya-
nashiro, Mami-chan's fan—friends with Morishita? Knew
about Morishita? Accomplice?" Without so much as thinking, I snatched that notebook from him.

"What's this?"

I flipped the pages and saw Aoyama's phone number and
address, "same group on class trip," my name, Mami Aino's
name. My eyes landed on my name and Aoyama's circled a
bunch of times, and I saw that Okayama had written "survivors" there. That's right. For some reason, somehow, we were
saved by Morishita. We were overlooked. Even though we
were in the same group as Tae-chan and Yamashiro.

"Give that back." Okayama quickly took back his notebook.

"This…"

"What? Are you going to tell me it's disgusting that I'm
wandering around looking this stuff up? I have a right to
know. To know what kind of people you are, what kind of
person Morishita is, what kind of personalities you all have,
what kind of lives you lived, how terrible Morishita is, how
cowardly, how he was a stuck-up punk who would do anything to get his hands on Mami-chan. In fact, you two have
a duty to tell me. If you've got the time to talk to the media, first you should call me. You shouldn't be putting on this
friendship act. Your whole youth was a mistake. It's your fault
for not stopping Morishita. Take responsibility and tell me
the truth. You and you both."

"It's not an act." Aoyama spoke weakly but clearly.

"What? What are you saying?"

"I was speaking honestly."

"Honestly? You're really saying that honestly he was a good

Astral Season, Beastly Season

guy? He killed her! He killed Minori. Minori wasn't supposed to be killed. She said mean things, but she was a nice girl, and she respected our mom. That's right. You know? Minori was actually the good one. So why? Why did he kill her? Why did he? Why did she have to die? It's so sad! Minori's life was so sad!"

Okayama's voice was trembling. He looked like even he didn't understand why it was shaky, why his tears were overflowing. He looked like he might even start crying blood. But still, Aoyama bit his lip and glared at him.

"You're just sad because your sister was killed. It's probably true that my words hurt you, but that doesn't make me a liar. I said what was true to me. You can't just deny my entire past. You say you're investigating, but will that get rid of your sadness? Won't meeting people like me just make you even angrier? I have things I want to protect, too. They may not look like anything important. They may not compare to the weight of someone's life. The only thing that's for sure here is we'll never really be able to talk to each other."

I couldn't bring myself to listen to Aoyama and Okayama speaking any more. Survivor. That word was burned into the backs of my eyes. We were survivors. We easily could have been killed. Aoyama was the one closest to Morishita. And I spent a lot of time with Morishita, too. *What even is this? What is it?* My body stiffened with cold as though a lump of ice had somehow crept into my heart. I was on the verge of tears. Even though it's all meaningless. Even though I don't get it. *What should I do? If I cry right here like this, it'd be such a nuisance to Aoyama and Okayama.*

Then, I remembered. One time on our class trip, Yamashiro made a face like I must be making now. On the bus, sitting next to Morishita. For some reason he started crying. I made some stupid excuse for him and said he was carsick and rubbed his back. But I couldn't understand why he was crying. I thought he really had no sense of how to act in public, so it would have been meaningless to tease him for crying. Why didn't I ask him what he was feeling then? What did Morishita say to him? Morishita must have made him cry. I had never seen him make anyone cry before. Why? What did Yamashiro know? Did he know much more about Morishita than I did?

"Why was it Yamashiro?" My mouth moved on its own.
"What?"
"Why not Aoyama?"
For some reason, I was shaking. The trembling was like loneliness, and it made me think, *This can't be.* But my skin was shaking, and my eyebrows scrunched themselves together. Why Tae-chan and not me? Why did Morishita decide he wanted us to live? Or, why didn't he want to kill us? I don't know. I don't think he really considered us individually. If he did, he wouldn't have killed Tae-chan. He wouldn't have killed Yamashiro either.

Aoyama made a totally worried face. Then he looked down like a child. I heard him say, "I don't know."
"What's wrong?" I asked.
"I was never into idols, but I would've gone to a concert if Morishita invited me. But I didn't know anything about this until afterwards. After he was arrested, I learned about it on

Astral Season, Beastly Season

the news. Why wasn't it me? That was the first thing I thought when Morishita got arrested. Didn't I mean anything to him?"

"Aoyama?"

"Morishita got arrested. He killed people. Still, I couldn't get that thought out of my head. I was so stupid for thinking he was my friend."

But, maybe, he wanted you to keep on living. I couldn't say anything like that. It wasn't true. Definitely not true. Morishita really always was a good guy. And Aoyama knew that better than anyone else. Morishita was fair. He wouldn't protect anyone, and he wouldn't kill anyone specific. He could only kill anyone because he didn't care if he killed everyone. He just killed whoever was there. We all knew he was a good guy. He wouldn't discriminate.

"But isn't it good that you weren't killed?"

Did that mean nothing to Aoyama? Was it more important to be chosen by Morishita? Once in elementary school there was this big scene because Aoyama hit Morishita with a recorder. When I looked into the classroom, Aoyama was on top of Morishita, punching him, a broken recorder next to them. Everyone said it was Aoyama's fault, but no one understood why he did it.

"What happened to Aoyama-kun?"

"He said that he was mad because Morishita wouldn't be in his group for the class trip."

"Really?"

"Morishita-kun already promised Na-chan he'd join her group."

"Aoyama's such a girl."

"Right? He's so lame."

All the girls made fun of him and crinkled their faces up laughing. Even though Morishita was right there in front of us getting beaten up. Aoyama was the one hitting Morishita, he was in a superior position to Morishita, but still, everyone looked at him with pity. "Aoyama-kun's just like that," someone said. "They call that kind of person goldfish poo," I heard someone say. "Always stuck to someone's behind." I hated the way people talked behind others' backs. I thought that was far, far more pathetic than Aoyama beating up Morishita. But I guess I became just as bad as them the moment I failed to shout that out loud. I couldn't be like Aoyama.

"Why did you ditch me! I wanted to go to Nagano with you!"

I thought Aoyama was amazing for being able to shout his real thoughts like that.

"Did you tell Morishita?" I asked Aoyama. He was hanging his head.

"They wouldn't let me see him."

I figured he would be somewhere no one could see him.

"I see." I rubbed Aoyama's back. "Let's go tell him someday. Morishita will get out soon. I'm sure he'll tell you why."

I knew my words were too blunt.

"Hey." It was Okayama. "You."

"Yes," I answered.

"What do you mean he'll get out soon?"

"Nothing," I said.

"He killed her! Minori is dead."

"Yes," I know.

Astral Season, Beastly Season

right away, "He left." I apologized for leaning on Aoyama's shoulder.

"I'm sorry," I said.

"Don't worry about it."

"But still."

"Not that. The things he said."

But I thought Okayama was right. I had been wrong.

"It's not like you need to be right. It was insensitive to say that in front of him, though."

He continued after a pause.

"But thanks. You saved me. I appreciate it."

The evening sun was falling on Aoyama's face, turning it red. *It's like fire*, I thought. I had seen this same sky a long time ago. When was it?

"Aoyama, you're smiling."

"Huh?"

"It's been a long time since I've seen your smile."

"Is that so?"

There's no need to be right. People will watch us. They will definitely hear us. And they will be hurt by our mistakes. Why is it, why do I want to tell Aoyama all this? I want to tell him this, but I can't say these things to myself. I think that distinction's very important. *It's fine to not be right. That goes for you, too. I was wrong, so Okayama yelled at me. Because I was wrong, Okayama was really hurt. But, Aoyama, like you said, it's fine, even if I'm not right. I just want you to say whatever you feel.*

"Aoyama, did you go to see him by yourself?"

"Yeah."

"Did you talk to anyone about it."

Astral Season, Beastly Season

"She was just fourteen. She was way younger than you. And she was killed by your friend. And what? He'll be out soon? What is that? I want him to hurry up and kill himself. I'm allowed to be that mad. It's normal. If he gets out of jail, I'll kill him. That's normal. I'm Minori's big brother. It's normal. He killed my sister because he wanted some stupid idol all to himself. Because of his desire, he killed Minori. He should die. He should die. And then what? He'll get out and then what? You tell him too. Tell Morishita to die. Send him a letter telling him to die. 'Die. Kill yourself. Get some rope.' What do you two want? Get over yourselves. You've never seen a photo of any of the bodies have you? You don't know what he did to them. You didn't see what was spread out all around here. He killed five people. Right here in this town where you live, on top of this grass, under this tree, he killed someone and left them. He tore up the bodies, he took off Minori's clothes, cut her skin, broke her bones and spread her all over. He did. Him! You. Hey! Don't you get it?"

"Ah." I heard a small yelp spill from me, and before it hit the ground, I felt my ankle twist. Someone was supporting my back. Probably Aoyama, I thought. "I'm sorry." Then my head felt the coldest it's ever been. Brrrr.

"So this is what it's like to have the blood drain from your head," I whispered, sitting next to Aoyama that evening. I had fainted, and apparently Aoyama waited by my side until I woke up.

When I finally came to, Okayama was gone. I thought for a moment he was just a character in a dream, but Aoyama said

"Just talking about Morishita freaks everyone out."

"Oh, yeah."

Right now, Morishita is at a place called a youth medical center. And Aoyama said that only parents are allowed to visit the people there.

"I went to see Morishita's dad, but I guess seeing someone like me just made him worry about all kinds of things... I'm so sorry for him. He's overwhelmed by thinking about Morishita and the families of the victims. But still he's doing his best. So I thought it would be wrong for me to go out of my way to try to meet him again... And also, for some reason, I thought if I went to see him, he'd die. And I couldn't do that to Morishita."

"Won't Morishita's situation change when he becomes an adult?"

"Will it?"

"Won't he leave the youth center? And go to a regular prison or something. I don't know, but I'll look into it. When he does, let's go see him again together."

"Yeah, thank you."

Aoyama was smiling. He was totally exhausted, but still, he was smiling. We're meaningless. We're not right. We didn't bring anyone back, we made Okayama angry, we're stupid. We have to go apologize. Apologize for all our mistakes.

"Aoyama, are you going to apply to the University of Kyoto?"

"I'm not sure. If you want me to go to the University of Tokyo, I can apply there."

"What are you saying?" I laughed. But still, Aoyama didn't look upset.

If I ever do get to meet Morishita again, will I have any-thing to say? I think I probably won't. But Aoyama's going to try to see him. I think I like that. I want to be with him. When that time comes, I want to be next to him. Fall will be here soon. The season everything happened. Maybe sometimes I'll talk to Aoyama about Morishita, and Aoyama will study hard for entrance exams. I'm sure.

"Hey, Aoyama?"

"Yeah?"

"Back in high school, I liked you, right?"

"Huh? Yeah."

Aoyama didn't look at me. He just rubbed his nose.

"Well, when Morishita got arrested, you know I was happy that you survived."

It seemed like the plants were dissolving into the air.

The summer night smelled like life ascending.

Afterword to the Season of Seventeen

When we were in school, we comforted ourselves by criticizing each other, saying who was right and who was wrong in
voices so soft no one else could hear us from where they were
positioned. Absolutely no one was right, and high school
wasn't anyone's ideal environment. But while the fact that we
were incomplete, that we were undecided, led to a sense of
discomfort, it also appeared to be a sort of guarantee—we
could use that as an excuse to thrash about as much as we
wanted.

That your classmates have never even heard of your favorite artist. That they've barely touched any works of literature.
That they know nothing about love. We looked down on others for plenty of reasons. I, too, judged others and was judged,
and it was through that process that we won our identities. I
know a lot about music. I know about love. I can study. In the
end, it really doesn't matter what kind of person you were
back in your school days. Everyone looked down on someone else to make themselves feel better. Thinking, *I'm differ-*

ent, was, more than anything else, our greatest commonality.

When do we first realize that youth is, or was, a season of discrimination? Where do we first find that out? It's the most nostalgic part of youth because it is itself a sign of our foolishness. To want to criticize others, to look down on others all just to be confident in yourself. Youth is a mess of a season, impossible to live through without criticizing both the self and others. But in youth we criticize both ourselves and others in their full humanity. It's only lonely adults that call others less than human.

Afterword to the Paperback Edition

Maybe there's no such thing as truly feeling alive. One day I just suddenly felt that way. I froze where I was standing. I could see my classmates running, their skirts fluttering above their white legs. *Maybe they don't understand the true meaning of "being alive,"* I thought. If you love, if you love deeply, and allow all to be as it is, then, finally, you may be able to see the threads of life that desperately tie together that flesh and blood and bone. Then you'll be able to understand, *Wow, I'm really alive.*

I don't like everyone enough to achieve that, I thought. *They don't like me that much, either.* When I realized that, I grew suddenly sad.

I had probably always considered myself to be alive. If I hadn't, why would I have kept on doing all these things that led to me getting hurt and hurting others? After spending a little time apart from even a close friend, their very existence seemed to be uncertain. A musician I love died. I felt myself listening to their music as though it was more precious than before their death, and that made me feel so sick I got scared. Value realized through loss cannot be true value. Still, there are things I only realize after losing something. I have no choice but to go on living this life through approximations, without knowing it all, missing the point again and again. I doubt myself because I say so easily that life is precious. I have no choice but to doubt myself.

Still yet, back then I felt that one day, one day I would find my own life. Just my own life. Regardless of what happens, the world is body temperature, and I faintly believed that even if it were the kind of cold place that simply forgets those who pass on, I would be able to figure out my life by seeing myself as its home, as its outline. And for that reason, I could stay in that freezing cold and continue to reach for something. I couldn't imagine those who live, who truly live. As I continued this process called living, I was overcome with unease at the thought that I was only dipping my feet in the clear top layer of life while everything else was sunk down to the bottom. Still yet, I thought that only those people who tried to capture life itself were truly being realistic.

The lives of the characters in this story are burning up within their bodies. They certainly cannot expose those lives to others, and no one will understand them fully. The world is a cold place, and without question, interpreting that coldness as pain is itself a form of arrogance. I want to continue to write characters who set their fingertips aflame with that arrogance and continue to reach for something.

Astral Season, Beastly Season

honfordstar.com